DON'T LOSE THIS BET!

"Stevie has come up with a brilliant idea," Lisa announced.

"What?" asked Carole nervously, afraid that the idea was going to be something that would create more aggravation among the three of them.

Lisa and Stevie twittered for a moment. Then Stevie burst out, "Simon Atherton!"

"Whichever one of us breaks our resolution first has to call up Simon and ask him out on a date!" Lisa said.

Lisa and Stevie watched to see how Carole would react. Slowly Carole began to grin. First she grinned a little, then a lot. "I can tell you one thing: I sure as heck am not going to be the one to lose!"

THE SADDLE CLUB

HORSE BLUES

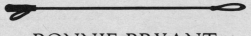

BONNIE BRYANT

A SKYLARK BOOK
NEW YORK · TORONTO · LONDON · SYDNEY · AUCKLAND

RL 5, 009–012

HORSE BLUES

A Bantam Skylark Book / January 1997

ISBN 0-553-48417-6

Published simultaneously in the United States and Canada.

Bantam Books are published by Bantam Books, a division of Bantam Dou-
bleday Dell Publishing Group, Inc. Its trademark, consisting of the words
"Bantam Books" and the portrayal of a rooster, is Registered in U.S. Patent
and Trademark Office and in other countries. Marca Registrada. Bantam
Books, 1540 Broadway, New York, New York 10036.

PRINTED IN THE UNITED STATES OF AMERICA

OPM   0 9 8 7 6 5 4 3 2 1

*I would like to express my special thanks
to Caitlin Macy for her help
in the writing of this book.*

1

"ISN'T IT MIDNIGHT YET?" Carole Hanson asked, stifling a yawn. It was New Year's Eve, and Carole and her two best friends, Stevie Lake and Lisa Atwood, were sacked out in front of the Hansons' TV. A sleepover was always fun, but this holiday evening seemed to be lacking something—excitement, maybe. Christmas was over, it was cold out, and Carole and Lisa, who went to the public school, had to go back the day after next. Stevie's private school had one more week off.

"Nice try, Carole," Stevie said, with a glance at her watch, "but it's not even eleven-thirty."

"You're not falling *asleep*, are you, Carole?" Lisa asked, feigning surprise.

"Oh, no," Carole insisted, "I'm wide awake."

Lisa and Stevie looked at their friend and laughed. Despite what she said, Carole's eyes were half closed and, up to this point, she hadn't said a word in half an hour. Stevie loved any excuse to stay up all night. Lisa was used to studying late when she had to. But Carole went to bed early. She enjoyed getting a good night's rest because she liked getting up early and spending as much time as possible with her horse, Starlight.

"Here, have some more soda," Lisa suggested. "It's got caffeine in it. That'll help you stay awake."

"I'm awake! I'm awake!" Carole protested. She sat up on the couch and took the can of cola Lisa handed her. "I really shouldn't drink this, you know," she said. "I eat way too much junk food."

Stevie raised her eyebrows. "You're not going to start worrying about your diet, are you?"

"I guess not," Carole said. "But sometimes I think I'd feel healthier if I didn't eat so much popcorn, chips, dip, cookies, candy—all the stuff my dad likes to snack on when we watch movies."

"Did I hear someone say *dad*?" The girls turned as Carole's father, Colonel Hanson, poked his head into the den. "I thought you girls might need a pick-me-up, so I brought you some buttered popcorn and a plate of nachos and salsa."

Carole groaned good-naturedly while Lisa and Stevie cheered.

"Colonel Hanson, did I ever tell you I like your style?" Stevie joked, eyeing the snacks appreciatively.

Carole's father beamed. "Oh, once or twice, Stevie, but it's still nice to hear." Colonel Hanson and Stevie had a special bond. They both loved old fifties movies, they both loved bad jokes, and they both loved junk food.

"Dad, why don't you join us?" Carole asked. "We're going to watch the ball drop in Times Square at midnight."

"If Carole can stay awake till then," Stevie said, needling her.

"Thanks, honey, but if you can believe it, I think I'm going to turn in now," Colonel Hanson said.

"Turn in? Half an hour before midnight?" Stevie asked, aghast.

Colonel Hanson chuckled. "I know, I know—but when you've seen as many midnights as I have, you can afford to miss one now and then. And we've all got to get up early for Horse Wise tomorrow."

Carole, Lisa, and Stevie rode and took lessons at Pine Hollow Stables. The owner of Pine Hollow, Max Regnery, had started Horse Wise, the local branch of the United States Pony Club. He held most of the mounted and unmounted meetings at his stable. The girls knew that Max really believed in Pony Club. He thought it was a great organization because it taught its members horsemanship and teamwork as well as riding skills. All three of the girls had participated widely in Horse Wise, earning higher ratings as they improved and competing in different events, including rallies, mounted games, and Know-Downs, which were quiz games about horses.

"So you're going tomorrow, too?" Lisa asked Colonel Hanson. "I know my mother is planning to be there."

"Yes, Max specifically asked the parents to come. I'm not sure why, but I guess we'll find out tomorrow," Colonel Hanson said. "I thought about asking Max when he called, but I didn't want to jump the gun."

Carole flashed her father a smile. At the beginning of Horse Wise, Carole's father had gotten so involved in the club—without knowing the first thing about horses—that he'd driven Carole crazy.

But since then, he'd kept his participation to a level that was acceptable to them both. He volunteered his time when Max needed him, but he didn't try to take over.

"I'm going to hit the hay now, so make sure you greet the New Year for me, okay, girls?"

"Will do, Dad—and thanks," Carole said, hugging her father good night.

The girls dug into the nachos.

"It's strange that Max invited the parents to a Horse Wise meeting," Lisa said thoughtfully.

"I think it was more of a command than an invitation," Carole remarked. "My dad said that when he talked to Max on the phone, Max's voice had a downright military ring to it."

"And your dad should know," Lisa said with a grin. Carole's father was a colonel in the United States Marine Corps.

"I'll bet Max wants to tell us what a great club we are and what exciting stuff we'll be doing in the new year," Stevie predicted, with typical optimism.

Lisa and Carole gave Stevie skeptical looks. Max Regnery was hardly the kind of person to call meetings just to give compliments. Even in riding lessons, his praise was kept to a minimum—just enough to let his students know they were making progress and little enough to let them know there was a lot of progress yet to be made.

"I doubt it, Stevie," said Lisa, "but since it's New Year's Eve, I'll look on the bright side."

"Speaking of the bright side," Carole began hopefully, "it's getting pretty late, right? Morning's just around the corner. Maybe we should—"

"No way! Not on your life, Carole Hanson," Stevie interrupted. "You're staying up till midnight if we have to—to make you start reciting equine trivia!"

"Now, there's an idea," said Carole, brightening. "All this New Year's stuff is boring."

"You said it," Lisa agreed. "I think New Year's is overrated, too. We're old enough to stay up, but we're too young to go out. Still, I'm glad I'm here instead of at my house. Right about now my mother would be telling me to get my 'beauty rest' or practice my embroidery."

"Practice your what?" Carole asked. Lisa's mother was constantly suggesting ways that Lisa could "improve" herself, but this was the first she'd heard of Lisa's learning embroidery.

"Yes, it's my mom's latest thing: She thinks it would be useful for me to learn the 'home arts'— knitting, crocheting, needlepoint—the works. I'm supposed to start with embroidery. Mom gave me needles, thread, and a book of patterns for Christmas. It looks more complicated than algebra. I'm supposed to be learning in my spare time. What I want to know is *what* spare time!" she exclaimed, exasperated. A straight-A student, Lisa was a perfectionist about her schoolwork. She also did her chores without complaining, kept her room perfectly neat, and generally did whatever her mother asked. All of that could add up to a lot of pressure.

"We saved you from home ec for a night, so at least this New Year's Eve has one thing to its credit," Carole said.

"*One* thing? What's wrong with you guys?" Stevie demanded. "TV? Junk food? Who could ask for anything more!"

Carole and Lisa laughed. Stevie had a great appreciation for the simple pleasures in life. She also had a great appreciation for creating elaborate plans and schemes. Sometimes she got so eager about them that she ended up dragging Lisa and Carole into crazy situations. But usually she could talk—or plan—her way right back out, no matter how complicated the mess she had created was. And being friends with Stevie was so much fun that Lisa and Carole didn't mind the occasional mix-up.

7

The three girls had been friends for a long time. Originally they had shared only a common love for horses, but now they also shared many past experiences and adventures. They were the core members of The Saddle Club, a group that they had started when they had first become friends. Members had to be two things: horse-crazy and willing to help each other out whenever possible.

As they snacked, Lisa tried to figure out a way she could make this boring New Year's Eve more fun.

As if she'd read Lisa's thoughts, Stevie said, "I have to admit, there's one person who I'll bet is having more fun than we are."

Judging by the annoyed tone in her voice, Lisa and Carole knew that Stevie could be referring to only one person: Veronica diAngelo. Veronica was a snobby girl who took lessons with The Saddle Club at Pine Hollow. She was also a member of Horse Wise, though she usually managed to avoid any work members had to do. None of The Saddle Club really liked Veronica, but she was Stevie's arch-enemy. Stevie and Veronica had so many ongoing feuds that nobody could keep track of them.

"So what's Miss diAngelo doing tonight?" Lisa inquired.

"Yeah, it must be something great if she was able

to tear herself away from all of the Christmas presents she's been bragging about," Carole added.

For the past week, every time the girls had seen Veronica at Pine Hollow, she had mentioned yet another expensive gift her parents had given her.

"Tonight *was* one of her Christmas presents," Stevie said enviously. "Her parents are taking her and a friend on a helicopter ride over the city."

The girls lived outside Washington, D.C., in a suburb called Willow Creek, Virginia. They had all taken field trips to museums or cultural events in D.C., but it was just like the diAngelos to give their daughter an extravagant gift like a private helicopter ride there on New Year's Eve.

"I wonder what 'friend' she bribed to go with her," Stevie muttered.

"Now, now," Lisa chided Stevie, putting on her best schoolmarm voice. "Thinking about Veronica isn't going to make our New Year's any more fun."

"You're right about that," Stevie agreed. "I was in a great mood till I remembered she existed."

"Hey, it's almost midnight!" Carole interrupted. "Ten minutes to go."

Lisa followed Carole's glance to the VCR clock above the television. *Ten more minutes, ten more minutes . . .* Suddenly she had an idea. "I've got it!" she exclaimed. "Let's make New Year's resolutions! We can write them on scraps of paper and throw them into the—well, we don't exactly have a fire to throw them into, but we can at least write them down."

"That's a great idea!" said Carole.

Now it was Stevie's turn to look doubtful. "Resolutions? You mean, like, vowing we're going to change? That doesn't sound like much fun."

"Sure it is! Making resolutions is the perfect thing to usher in the New Year. I can't believe we didn't think of them before," said Lisa.

"I can," said Stevie under her breath.

Carole sat up on the couch, fully awake at last. "What do you think we should resolve?" she asked, cracking open another soda.

Lisa smiled. "I can think up a resolution for you, Carole."

Carole paused, the can halfway to her lips. "Yeah? What?"

"No more junk food," said Lisa.

Carole winced. She put the can back down. "No more junk food," she repeated.

"You said yourself you eat too much of it," Lisa pointed out. "This is a great opportunity to stop."

Carole thought hard for a minute. Why not? Why not stop talking about quitting junk food and do something about it? "You know, you're right. I'll do it. I'll make it my New Year's resolution: I resolve to quit eating junk food." *There*, Carole thought, *that was easy.*

"You have to write it down," Lisa reminded her.

"Oh, right," Carole said. She chewed her lip. She didn't really feel like writing it down. It made it seem so much more real. But she'd come this far. Lisa was watching her expectantly. "Okay," she said. She reached over and grabbed some notepaper and a pen from the table beside the couch. It was only a resolution, after all. It wasn't written in stone.

"Okay, I'm done," Carole pronounced, after spelling out her vow. "Who's next? How about you, Stevie?"

"Yeah, Stevie, come on. What do you want to resolve?" Lisa prompted.

Stevie smiled wanly. "To tell you the truth, I'm happy with myself just the way I am," she said. "I don't think I need to change a thing."

"Really?" Lisa challenged her. "Because I can think of a great resolution for you, too."

"Oh? Can you?" Stevie replied. Somehow she had a feeling she wasn't going to like Lisa's suggestion. But Carole was watching Lisa, and Lisa was looking eagerly at Stevie. Stevie sighed. "All right. Let's hear it."

Lisa smiled approvingly. "Resolve to be nice to Veronica."

"What?" Stevie nearly yelled. "Why would I want to do a thing like that?" Being nice meant not being mean, and not being mean to Veronica was like . . . like not breathing!

"Well, for one, it's a waste of time. Think of all the things you could be doing that you don't do because you're scheming of ways to get back at Veronica," said Lisa.

Stevie thought for a minute. She couldn't think of anything. "I'm not as tightly scheduled as you, Lisa. I have plenty of time in my day for getting back at Veronica," she joked.

"Okay, okay—but what about Max?" Lisa said. "He'd be really happy if you two stopped feuding."

Stevie nodded. "I guess so . . ." She knew Lisa was right. In the past, her fights with Veronica had sometimes made life difficult for Max and everyone at Pine Hollow. But could she quit being mean to

Veronica just like that? Cold turkey? "But what if *Veronica* tries to fight with *me*?"

"Stevie," Carole spoke up. She thought she had a better way than Lisa's to convince Stevie. "I know something that might make you want that for a resolution."

"What's that?" Stevie asked suspiciously. She didn't like the feeling that Carole and Lisa were ganging up on her.

"You want to win your fights with Veronica, right? You want to come out on top? Well, my dad says that sometimes the only way to win is not to fight. You know, not to respond at all. If Veronica can't provoke you, that might make her really mad."

Lisa nodded in agreement. "She's right, Stevie. Imagine how annoyed Veronica will be when she insults you and all you do is smile at her."

"Imagine how annoyed *I'll* be!" Stevie wailed. But Carole and Lisa did have a point. Where Veronica was concerned, Stevie had hardly ever tried the method of killing with kindness. "Okay," she said finally, "you talked me into it. I hereby resolve to quit being mean to Veronica diAngelo." Stevie took the paper and pen and wrote her resolution underneath Carole's.

"Two minutes to midnight!" Lisa exclaimed.

"Better make your resolution fast, Lisa," Stevie said pointedly.

Lisa looked surprised at Stevie's sharp tone. "All right, all right—let me think of something."

"No, why don't you let Carole and me think of something, since you thought of ours?" Stevie suggested.

"But—" Lisa began.

"Good idea, Stevie," Carole agreed. "After all, it's only fair. Let's see . . ."

"I know," Stevie said, an impish light in her eyes. "Lisa, why don't you resolve to learn embroidery, since your mother wants you to so much?"

"But I—well—" Lisa stopped. The idea of learning embroidery was utterly repulsive to her. She had been planning to put it off for as long as she could.

It was 11:59. Stevie and Carole were waiting. It wouldn't be fair to back down now. "Fine!" Lisa said defensively. "Embroidery it is. Give me the pen."

Carole and Stevie watched over Lisa's shoulder as she wrote down her resolution.

"Twenty seconds to midnight!" Carole pointed to the TV, where the ball was dropping in New York City's Times Square. Together the girls counted down the last seconds. "Ten, nine, eight, seven, six, five, four, three, two, one! Yea!" they yelled.

"Let's toast the New Year!" Stevie urged. All three of them picked up their sodas and prepared to drink.

"Uh, Carole?" Lisa murmured, pointing at the can in Carole's hand.

Carole frowned. "Oh, right. Hold on. I'll, um . . . get some water."

"Can't she even have one sip of soda?" Stevie asked, annoyed.

Lisa shrugged. "Don't look at me. *I* don't care. But a resolution is a resolution."

THE AIR AT Pine Hollow the next morning was buzz-
ing with something, though it wasn't exactly excitement. Max Regnery had assembled the active
members of Horse Wise and their parents. Stevie's
parents couldn't make the meeting because they
were visiting out-of-town friends for the day. Mrs.
Atwood had come as promised, however. And Colonel Hanson had arrived with a very sleepy Lisa,
Stevie, and Carole. The tack room was packed with
riders and parents waiting for Max to bring the
meeting to order.

"It looks like most of the members showed up,"

Carole observed, glancing around the crowded room.

"Most—but not all," Stevie noted dryly. "Veronica's probably too tired from her helicopter tour of the city to come to something as boring as an unmounted Horse Wise meeting."

"Stevie . . . ," Lisa said warningly.

Stevie shot Lisa an annoyed look. "Look, I resolved not to be mean to Veronica," she snapped. "That doesn't mean I can't talk about her behind her back."

Lisa was about to respond when her mother appeared in front of them. "Hi, honey. Hi, girls. Happy New Year," said Mrs. Atwood. "How was the slumber party?"

"It was fun, Mom. We—"

"It was great!" Stevie said, jumping in. "Lisa told us that she almost stayed home because she wanted to work on her embroidery, but you're glad you came, aren't you, Lis'?" Stevie's hazel eyes glinted tauntingly.

"Did you say that, honey?" asked Mrs. Atwood, obviously pleased.

Lisa glared at Stevie before recovering herself. "Yes, Mom. I can't wait to start," she said through clenched teeth.

"Wonderful! I wasn't sure if you liked your Christmas present, but I'm so glad you do! Thank you for telling me, Stevie. Perhaps you and Carole would like to join Lisa. All girls should know how to embroider, you know."

"Thanks, Mrs. Atwood, but . . ." Stevie paused, trying to think up an excuse.

"Yes, thank you, but I'm going to be busy learning how to cook," Carole cut in.

"Are you, dear? That's wonderful, too. What are you going to make?" Mrs. Atwood inquired.

Lisa and Stevie looked at Carole curiously. They had no idea what she was getting at. Carole grinned. "Oh, I'll be making nutritious meals—vegetable casseroles, salads, sugar-free desserts . . ."

Lisa and Stevie laughed, both relieved that Carole had changed the subject from embroidery to her own resolution.

"That's nice, Carole," Mrs. Atwood said vaguely. "It's always good to eat healthy food."

"Healthy food?" Colonel Hanson asked, coming over to greet Lisa's mother. "Yuck! I say, keep your alfalfa sprouts for the rabbits and give me a burger, fries, and a Coke any day of the week. Happy New Year, Eleanor."

As Mrs. Atwood and Colonel Hanson shook

hands and began to chat, Stevie, Lisa, and Carole drifted away. It was bad enough having their parents present at a Horse Wise meeting: They didn't want to talk to them, too!

"Am I crazy, or is Max actually late?" Stevie asked when the three of them were settled on the floor in a corner. The talking had reached a higher pitch as the group waited for the meeting to start.

"You *are* crazy, as we all know, Stevie," Carole kidded, "but you're right, too. Max is fifteen minutes late." She pointed to the tack room clock. "The meeting was supposed to start at nine."

Lisa's eyes grew big. "This might be the first time in Pine Hollow history that Max has been late," she murmured.

"I can't believe it. I just can't believe it," Stevie breathed, awestruck. For as long as she could remember, Stevie had been getting into trouble with Max for showing up late to meetings. Now it seemed that the tables had finally turned.

"Do you think something happened?" Carole asked, worried.

"Yeah, maybe his alarm clock didn't work, or the dog ate his homework," Stevie suggested, laughing at the idea of Max using two of her favorite excuses.

Carole gave her a withering glance. "No, seriously—it's strange for him to be late," she said. "I hope he's not sick."

Before the girls could wonder any longer, the tack room door flew open and Max entered. Strangely enough, he didn't seem at all perturbed or apologetic about being late. Nor did he seem in a big hurry to start the meeting. He sauntered toward the front of the room, pausing to chat with different students and parents on the way.

Astonished, Stevie stared at the owner of Pine Hollow Stables. She'd been sure that he would hurry in and call the meeting to order immediately. Maybe, she thought suddenly, his watch had stopped, and he had no idea how late he was! How embarrassing! "Max," she said in a stage whisper. "Max, over here!"

Max turned and waved hello. "Hi, Stevie! Happy New Year."

Stevie motioned wildly for him to forget the small talk. "It's almost nine-twenty!" she hissed.

Max looked at his wristwatch. "Ah, so it is. I guess I should start the meeting, shouldn't I?"

At that, The Saddle Club stared at one another in disbelief. Max prided himself on his organization and efficiency, as well as his respect for his students and their parents. Now he was behaving like the bad kid in school.

"Okay, what gives?" Carole whispered.

"I don't know, but I have the feeling we're about to find out," said Lisa.

"And it doesn't look good," Stevie muttered.

Max had finally made his way to the front of the room. But now instead of joking, his expression was grim. He held up a hand for silence, cleared his throat, and began.

"As some of you so kindly pointed out on my way in, this special meeting was supposed to start twenty minutes ago." Max paused dramatically. Then he continued, speaking clearly and emphasizing every word. "I came late on purpose—to show you what it's like to come on time only to find that someone else is late and holding up the whole meeting."

Stevie shifted uneasily in her seat. She knew that she had been that "someone else" more than a few times.

"That happens a lot at Horse Wise. Of course, if lateness were the only problem besetting this Pony Club, I wouldn't have much cause for concern. But it's the tip of the iceberg. Look around the room. It probably looks packed to you. But does anyone remember that a year ago I held meetings in the indoor ring because Horse Wise was too big to meet in the tack room?"

A few people nodded and murmured among themselves.

"Well, I do. The fact is, membership has fallen off. Some riders dropped out formally; others just stopped coming. And a few prefer mounted meetings to unmounted," Max added, under his breath.

The Saddle Club eyed one another. They knew Max meant Veronica. The girl was so spoiled that she didn't see the point in learning the horsemanship—grooming, conformation, and basic veterinary skills—that the unmounted meetings taught.

"And parents: I'm sorry to have to say this since so many of you made the effort to come today, but the truth is, parental support in this club is way, way down."

Now it was the parents who looked at one another guiltily, mumbling apologies and excuses, as Max let his words sink in.

"I understand that it's winter, and we're all less interested in riding now than we will be in three months. But winter is the time for us to get our act together for the spring rallies and other competitions." Max looked down at the clipboard he was holding and consulted a list. "At the very least, we must beg, borrow, or steal the following for the spring season of events: new matching saddle pads and cross-country hat covers; new tires on the two vans; money to pay whoever teaches our dressage clinic in April; entry fees for the events on our summer schedule. . . . I could go on, but I think you get the picture.

"Now, I don't want to make the situation sound worse than it is. This club has a lot of talent and dedication. But my mother and I have been working double time to fill in the gaps you all leave, and we can't anymore." Max gestured to his mother, Mrs. Reg, who was listening in the back of the room. Mrs. Reg was a favorite among The Saddle Club. It was no surprise that she had been helping Max run Horse Wise. She could always be counted on in a pinch. If The Saddle Club happened to be hanging out at Pine Hollow, Mrs. Reg would put them right to work cleaning tack, scrubbing buckets, or giving the stalls a once-over. She worked right beside them. If there was anyone whom they hated to disappoint more than Max, it was Mrs. Reg.

"And so," Max was saying, "after a lot of thinking, I've decided to put the club on trial for an indefinite period of time. You—all of you—are going to have to show me that you want this club as much as I do. If it turns out that that's not the case . . ." Max paused and cleared his throat, then continued, his voice strained with emotion, "then we've all learned a lot and had a good time up until now. At least," he added softly, "I know I have."

Lisa, Stevie, and Carole exchanged looks of dismay. None of them had missed the note of resignation in Max's voice. "He's really choked up!" Carole whispered.

In a moment, Max had regained his composure. He surveyed the room briefly, looked down at his notes one more time, then concluded, "That's really all I have to say. I've got horses to exercise, so I'll be on my way."

After Max left the room, there was a moment or two of stricken silence. Everyone seemed to realize that they had taken Max and Horse Wise for granted. Nobody seemed to know what to say. They were used to Max telling them what to do. Carole was lost in thought. Stevie knew that a joke at a time like this would be inappropriate. Lisa racked her brains, trying to think of something practical that would rally the Pony Clubbers and their parents.

"Excuse me?" a woman said timidly.

The group turned. It was Mrs. Atwood. Lisa did a double take. Usually Mrs. Atwood left the riding to Lisa and concentrated her energies on school fairs for the parent-teacher association. She wasn't like the mothers who knew about horses and helped look after their children's ponies. She looked out of place in the stables—even today she was wearing a wool suit and high heels. But, Lisa thought, listening to her mother's words, she *did* know a heck of a lot about organizing people.

"I don't know anything about horses," Mrs. Atwood began, "but from what Max said, it sounds to me as if the main thing we need right now is money. I have a suggestion for how to raise some. It's not a new idea, but it's simple and it's fast and it works."

"Yes, Mrs. Atwood?" one of the parents asked politely.

"We could have a bake sale," Lisa's mother said. "On a Saturday," she added. "At the Willow Creek shopping center."

Stevie raised her eyebrows. "Now, that's my kind of suggestion!" she murmured to Carole and Lisa.

Mrs. Atwood looked around the room. "So, do I have any takers?"

"I think that's a wonderful idea," Mrs. Reg responded immediately. "What does everyone else think?"

"Hear! Hear!" said Colonel Hanson.

Mrs. McLean, the mother of one of the younger girls in Horse Wise, spoke up. "I think that's a super plan. That way we could all get involved. Both Pony Clubbers and parents can bake things, and we can take turns manning the sale table."

"Can I make my famous double-fudge brownies?" said a woman from the back.

"Mom, I want to make peanut butter cookies!" a young boy piped up.

"I've got a German chocolate cake that will knock your socks off," Betsy Cavanaugh's mother boasted.

All at once, everyone was talking excitedly about the bake sale plans. Lisa looked at her mother with new appreciation. With one suggestion, she had turned everyone's mind from worrying to productive planning. No wonder she was such a hit at PTA meetings.

"This will be great," said Colonel Hanson to Carole. "We can have an all-day bake-a-thon!"

Carole smiled but grimaced inwardly. Like everyone else, she thought the idea of the bake sale was great. But why did it seem like all of a sudden, wherever she turned, there was junk food? "Sure, Dad, we can bake up a storm," she replied, trying to muster enthusiasm.

When Mrs. Atwood volunteered to organize the sale, Lisa thought happily of her New Year's resolution. It would be a perfect thank-you for Lisa to present her mother with a piece of embroidery . . . at some time in the very distant future!

"I say the sooner we can hand Max a check, the better," Mrs. Atwood was saying. "So why not have this sale on Saturday in two weeks? That ought to give us plenty of time."

"Boy, like mother, like daughter," Stevie commented, watching Mrs. Atwood start to take down volunteers' names.

"Yeah, I guess hyper-organization runs in the family," Lisa laughed.

As the meeting broke up, Lisa's mother started a sign-up sheet so that people could list their names, numbers, and the baked goods they wanted to bring. Before long, the sheet was practically full. Carole read down the list of food items: brownies, blondies, hermit cookies, fudge, lemon cake, devil's food cake—

"Here, Carole," a voice said.

Carole turned, glad to be distracted. The list of

baked goods was making her crave sweets. She looked up. It was Mrs. Reg, smiling warmly, holding out a tray of miniature doughnuts.

"Mrs. Reg?" said Carole, momentarily confused.

Mrs. Reg held the plate out closer to Carole. "I brought these for the meeting, so enjoy them, dear!"

AFTER THE MEETING, Stevie, Lisa, and Carole decided to go riding in the indoor ring. None of them could bear to come to Pine Hollow and not ride. They went their separate ways to groom and tack up Belle, Prancer, and Starlight.

While she was brushing Starlight, Carole thought about her resolution. She had already broken it by looking around guiltily for Stevie and Lisa and then eating half of a miniature honey-dipped doughnut and washing it down with cocoa. Mrs. Reg had looked so pleased with her offering that Carole hadn't known how to say no.

"Maybe sweets aren't the same as junk food, boy. What do you think?" Carole asked the bay gelding. She put down her currycomb and picked up a soft brush. Maybe desserts really belonged in their own category. And what about soda? Was that junk *food*? And hot chocolate? Those were drinks, so they couldn't count, could they?

"At least I can tell you, Star." Carole sighed. She knew she should, but Carole didn't want to admit to Lisa and Stevie that she had cheated. It seemed pathetic to fail on the very first day of the new year! Lisa and Stevie would think she had no willpower.

Carole sighed again as she laid the saddle gently on Starlight's reddish-brown back. "Imagine how you'd feel if you'd given up sweet feed and could eat nothing but boring old pellets and hay," she told the young Thoroughbred. Starlight swiveled his ears back and forth. "You horses are so lucky," Carole muttered. "You're too smart to make resolutions!"

IN THE RING, Stevie seemed to have had a similar thought. "I guess Belle didn't make any resolutions to behave," she said cheerfully. "She's pulling like a train!"

Stevie's horse, Belle, was an Arabian-Saddlebred

cross. Like Stevie, she was very feisty and spirited, sometimes even stubborn. She liked to go fast, too. "Whatever gait we're going, she wants to go one faster," Stevie commented, sitting down firmly in the saddle to settle the mare. "She wanted to trot so I let her, and now that we're trotting, she wants to canter. What do you think would happen if I let her gallop full out?"

"She'd probably take off, run around the ring, buck several times, tire herself out, and quit," Carole said seriously. "The problem is that if you let her take off once, she'd want to do it again, and then again, and pretty soon she'd be uncontrollable."

"Thanks, Carole," Stevie said with a touch of sarcasm. Carole was so passionate about horses that sometimes she failed to see when someone was only kidding. She was famous for her long-winded answers to horse-related questions.

Lisa came in leading Prancer, a bay Thoroughbred mare. Officially she was owned by Pine Hollow, but Lisa had long been her usual rider.

Lisa paused to tighten Prancer's girth and roll down her stirrups for mounting. "I would have been here sooner," she said, springing into the saddle, "but, thanks to you, Stevie, I had to spend ten minutes convincing my mother that I wanted to ride just as much as I wanted to go home and start embroidering."

Stevie and Carole laughed, and Lisa finally did too, but she didn't find the situation all that funny. She had made the resolution, and she would learn to embroider, but she didn't intend to make it a high priority. If her mother thought she was genuinely interested, she would be on her case even more than she usually was. It was typical of Stevie to tease without realizing what the consequences would be. Typical and annoying, Lisa thought, tightening her reins.

Lisa joined Stevie and Carole at the rail. Usually if they were riding in the ring at the same time, the three of them would school together, too, making up games for the others or helping one another with problems. But this morning, each of the girls seemed content to do her own thing. The combination of Max's lecture and the New Year's resolutions wasn't doing wonders for their camaraderie. Stevie stayed on the outside rail, practicing downward transitions from canter to trot, trot to walk, and walk to halt. Carole did bending exercises in a circle at the far end of the ring. And Lisa worked on her position, riding without stirrups at the trot and canter.

The three of them were concentrating so hard that they lost track of one another. All of a sudden, they ended up in the middle of the ring at the exact same time. "Heads up!" Carole cried, as both Belle and Prancer almost collided with Starlight.

By sitting up hard and snapping the reins, Lisa and Stevie managed to stop their horses short of a collision.

"That was a close one!" a woman's voice called. The girls turned in their saddles as Mrs. Reg entered the ring. "Do you have a minute?"

"Sure!" the three of them said in unison. It was funny, Lisa thought, but it was as if they were glad to have an outside person present—to break the tension between them.

"The bake sale was a great idea, don't you think?" Mrs. Reg asked, coming over to join them.

"The best!" said Stevie. "You're not going to tell Max, though, are you?"

Mrs. Reg feigned indignation. "What do you take me for? I knew you'd want it to be a secret until it's a done deed and you have the cash in hand, so to speak. Don't worry—my lips are sealed. I just came to tell you that, since I'm sure you three will have something to do with the organizing, I know a few riders who haven't been involved in Horse Wise recently but might be persuaded to help."

"And who could rejoin the club if they've let their memberships lapse?" Lisa asked.

"Precisely," said Mrs. Reg. She named a few students the girls remembered. "And finally, there's a certain boy who I'll bet would be a great help. He's been away for a while, but he's very enthusiastic."

"Who's that?" Stevie asked.

"His name is Simon Atherton. His father got temporarily transferred so he's been living in . . ."

None of The Saddle Club heard the end of Mrs. Reg's sentence. Lisa clapped her hand to her mouth. "Simon Atherton!" she wailed. "Oh, no!"

"Bet you thought you'd never see him again, huh, Lisa?" said Stevie, grinning.

"But I thought he'd quit riding forever," Carole added.

"Quit? No, he didn't quit," Mrs. Reg said brightly. "As I was saying, his father got transferred from Washington to Texas for a few months and took the whole family with him. Simon's been living in Houston. That's why you haven't seen him around."

Stevie, Lisa, and Carole groaned. Lisa groaned

the loudest. Then they remembered Mrs. Reg. She was trying to help. They were acting like a bunch of ungrateful jerks. "I'm sorry, Mrs. Reg," Lisa began, "it's just . . ." She paused, not knowing how to continue. How could they tell Max's mother that Simon Atherton was the last person on earth they wanted help from for the bake sale?

Simon was the nerdiest boy in Willow Creek. He had once had a huge crush on Lisa. He had followed her around, asking her if she wanted to study with him, solve math problems together, or do extra-credit homework. Even for Lisa, he was too goody-goody! But if what Mrs. Reg said was true, and Simon was ready and willing to help out, they couldn't avoid him. They had to put Horse Wise first.

Carole rushed to Lisa's aid. "Thanks, Mrs. Reg. We'll give him a call right away."

"All right, dears," Mrs. Reg replied happily.

Lisa breathed a sigh of relief. Mrs. Reg tended to be a little spacy. Luckily she didn't seem to have noticed the girls' initial reactions.

"By the way, girls," Mrs. Reg added, "have you seen the boarder in the stall next to Patch's?"

The three girls nodded, holding their breath to see if Mrs. Reg was going to leave off there or continue with one of her endless—and pointless—stories.

"You mean the chestnut, right?" Lisa asked.

"That's right, the chestnut. Pretty, isn't he?" said Mrs. Reg.

"Yes, Mrs. Reg, he's very pretty," Lisa replied. Now if only Mrs. Reg would leave it at that . . . !

Mrs. Reg turned to go. Then she turned back around. "A real beauty if you ask me. Of course, he's a European warmblood, so you would expect that. Did you know his owners imported him from Germany?"

Stevie jumped in. "No, Mrs. Reg. But he sure is a pretty horse."

"I'll say. But you should have seen him a year ago. He wasn't much to look at when the owners first bought him. As a yearling, he was downright unattractive. Some breeds mature slowly. It takes them a long time to come into their own. But once they do, they often have better conformation than the ones that start out attractive. Funny, isn't it?" Mrs. Reg mused.

Stevie fiddled conspicuously with her stirrups. Lisa fiddled with her reins. Carole cleared her throat.

"All right, I'll be on my way. You three had better get back to your riding." Mrs. Reg sighed. "My, that chestnut turned out nicely, though. . . ."

For the rest of their ride, the girls giggled to themselves. Mrs. Reg meant well, but she sure could ramble!

"OKAY, WHO'S UP for TD's?" Stevie queried. The horses had been rubbed down, and the girls were about to finish wiping off their tack. Stevie thought it was only fitting that they usher in the new year with a visit to their favorite ice cream parlor.

"Umm . . . I can't," Lisa confessed, to Stevie's surprise.

"Me either," Carole said glumly.

"This year is starting out awfully strange," Stevie said, shaking her head. "First Max comes purposefully late to a Horse Wise meeting, then Mrs. Reg tells a *short*, pointless story, and now you two are turning down a trip to Tastee Delight?"

"I promised my mother I'd go home and start my embroidery project right after we rode," Lisa explained. Mentally she added, *Which I wouldn't have had to do if you hadn't said anything, Stevie.*

Stevie looked down at the floor, wishing she

could take back her remark to Lisa's mother. "What's your excuse, Carole?" she asked. "Where do you have to be?"

Carole looked awkward. "It's just—well—I don't have to be anywhere. But if I go to TD's, I'll want to get ice cream, and I can't, since that's junk food."

Stevie glanced at her friends. "You know what I think? I think we should just . . ." Stevie paused. She could feel Lisa's eyes on her. She had been about to say, "I think we should just forget all about these silly resolutions." But Stevie didn't want to be the first one to quit. Lisa would think she had no self-discipline, that she only wanted to get out of her resolution. And why should she look bad? Being nice to Veronica was a piece of cake so far.

"You think we should just what?" Carole asked hopefully. She had an inkling of what was on Stevie's mind. If only Stevie would spit it out! Then she could tell them about eating the doughnut. They could laugh about it and forget these stupid resolutions.

"I think we should—I mean, I think *you* should come to TD's and—and order a diet soda or a fat-free frozen yogurt," Stevie finished lamely. "And Lisa, can't you call your mother and tell her you'll be an hour late? The embroidery can wait, can't it?"

"I don't know, can it?" Lisa said cryptically. She didn't want to look as if she was trying to cheat on her resolution, especially since the resolutions had been her idea in the first place.

"Of course it can!" Stevie said. "It's barely noon. You'll have all afternoon to embroider!"

Right, thought Lisa, *after I empty the dishwasher, set the table* . . . Still, she didn't want to be left out. "I'll go if you will, Carole," she said.

"We-e-ll, I guess so," Carole replied. If Lisa went to TD's, then wouldn't she sort of be cheating, too? Maybe she would keep putting off the embroidery and finally forget all about it. Then Carole could forget about not eating junk food!

Feeling relieved but still somehow uneasy, the girls hung up their bridles and saddles and headed for the door. As Carole opened it, Veronica di-Angelo flounced in. Veronica was dressed in new riding clothes from head (the newest-style velvet hunt cap) to toe (custom-made tall boots).

Before they could get a word in, Veronica started to talk a mile a minute. "Hello, girls! Did you have an exciting New Year's Eve? Mine was the best ever! I guess you heard I went on a helicopter ride over the city? It was just marvelous! Me, my family, and a special friend. We stayed out way past midnight. Of course, I'm sure watching TV or whatever boring, humdrum thing you and your little club did was fun in its way—"

"Aren't you running late, Veronica?" Stevie broke in abruptly, gritting her teeth. The nerve! People like Veronica were the reason Horse Wise was failing! Stevie would have liked to tell Veronica off, but she couldn't—at least not in front of Lisa and Carole.

"Late? Why, no," Veronica replied. "I don't think so. My jumping lesson with Johannes Wendt doesn't start till twelve-thirty. One of the stable hands should have Danny ready by now, so I'm actually early. But then, unlike you, I make it a point to be on time."

Stevie clenched her hands into fists. That was a low blow, and Veronica knew it. Stevie was already upset about her tardiness, but she didn't have maids to get her dressed and a chauffeur to drive her places and—

"You're having a lesson with Johannes Wendt?" Carole breathed. Wendt was a four-time German Equestrian Team member. When he taught in the United States, he reputedly charged a couple of hundred dollars an hour for lessons. Carole would have given the shirt off her back to ride with' him.

"I certainly am. It was one of my Christmas presents. Along with these European breeches, this jumping bat—"

"Okay, okay!" Stevie burst out. "We've heard enough about your presents! Did it ever occur to you that it's rude to brag all the time?"

Carole and Lisa were speechless. Stevie had broken her resolution right in front of them.

"Jealousy will get you nowhere, Stevie," Veronica said evenly.

"Jealousy? You listen to me! We had a Horse Wise meeting this morning. Not that you'd care since you hate anything involving teamwork, but—"

"Stevie?" Carole said hesitantly. She hated to interrupt, since what Stevie said was true, but she could tell Stevie had forgotten about her resolution in the heat of the moment. "Don't you think we'd better be going?" she asked gently.

All at once, Stevie seemed to remember herself. "Oh, yeah," she said quietly, embarrassed by her outburst. "You're right." She turned to follow Lisa and Carole out the door.

"Toodle-oo!" Veronica called cheerily after them.

"Happy New Year," Stevie muttered bitterly.

"YOU THREE ARE pretty darn quiet," the waitress at TD's observed. "Wha's a matter? Cat got your tongues?"

None of The Saddle Club bothered to respond. Carole stared glumly at her menu, trying to figure out what to order that wouldn't be junk food. Lisa fiddled nervously with her spoon. She had just returned from phoning her mother to tell her that she wouldn't be home until later. "But I thought you couldn't wait to start embroidering," Mrs. Atwood had said, making Lisa feel guilty.

Even Stevie's spirits were dampened by her run-in

with Veronica. Maybe urging Lisa and Carole to come had been a stupid idea after all. They certainly didn't seem too excited to be there.

"So, come on, come on, hurry up already. You think I got all day? What'll it be?" the waitress demanded, snapping her gum.

Carole thought fast. "I'll have a lemonade," she decided.

"A dish of vanilla ice cream, please," said Lisa. She wasn't in the mood for anything more elaborate.

"And I'll take a—a—" Stevie paused. She had been about to order one of her famous concoctions but decided against it. She thought it would be obnoxious to get a huge sundae when Carole was trying not to eat junk food.

As Stevie was debating with herself, however, Carole spoke up. "I know what you're thinking, and believe me, Stevie, the grosser the sundae you get, the better. I'm not likely to be tempted by peanut butter ice cream with strawberry sauce, you know!"

Lisa and Stevie laughed, and the waitress, who was used to Stevie's preferences for revolting sundaes, made a face.

"Hey, peanut butter and strawberry—that sounds good!" said Stevie, perking up. "I'll take it—plus a scoop of Oreo cookie, marshmallow topping, and a maraschino cherry."

As Carole and Lisa grimaced, the waitress turned to place their orders, shaking her head and muttering. "One of these days, boy, I'm going to run out of patience and you're going to get nothing but hot fudge on vanilla, ya hear me?"

The Saddle Club giggled.

When she returned, the waitress handed Carole the lemonade. "What are you, on some kind of a diet?" she asked, eyeing Carole suspiciously.

"Not exactly," Carole replied. She cast a baleful glance at Lisa and Stevie, hoping they would help her change the subject.

" 'Cause let me tell you, it won't work. I've tried 'em all—low-fat, no-fat, high-protein, grapefruit— you might as well forget about it. You'll just gain it all right back."

"Thanks for your advice," Carole said sarcastically.

"She's not on a diet," Lisa piped up. "She's trying to give up junk food."

The waitress looked momentarily impressed. "Now there's an idea. . . . Nah, that won't work either. It'll just make you crazy. Sure you don't want a chocolate cone?"

"Yes," Carole said testily. "I'm sure."

"Or a shake? A vanilla shake?"

"No, *thank you.*"

"Root beer float?"

"No!"

"Chipwich with—"

"*No!* Look, I'm happy with my lemonade, okay?" Carole burst out.

The waitress raised her eyebrows. She stepped back from the table. "Well, excu-u-use me," she said, turning on her heel.

"Don't mind her, Carole," Lisa murmured, seeing Carole's exasperated expression. "She's probably just jealous that you have the willpower and she doesn't."

"Yeah, boy, have you got willpower," Stevie said. She surveyed her sundae happily from all angles before digging in.

Carole grumbled something incoherent as she sipped her lemonade.

"What was that?" Lisa asked.

"I said, I don't have the willpower you think I do," Carole repeated. In a rush she told Stevie and Carole about breaking down and eating the doughnut earlier. The minute she said it, it seemed like the silliest thing in the world to get worked up about. Carole giggled as she finished, adding that she didn't know whether the hot chocolate "counted" or not. "Anyway, I felt bad not telling you guys, so . . ."

Stevie was the first to speak. "Uh, Carole? I wouldn't feel too bad, considering that I've already broken my resolution, too. You both saw me lose my temper with Veronica when she came waltzing in hours after the meeting was over."

Lisa nodded. "Right. And I should be home doing embroidery right now."

"Yes, but you haven't actually broken your resolution, Lisa," Carole pointed out.

"Well, that's because—" Lisa started to say.

"That's because hers is harder to break," Stevie finished.

Annoyed, Lisa put her spoon down and looked at Stevie. "What's that supposed to mean?"

"It's simple," Stevie replied. "Your resolution is harder to break because you vowed to learn something new, whereas we vowed to change habits that we already have; so to break ours, all Carole and I have to do is slip up and do it, whereas to not do yours all you have to do is not do something. I mean, to do yours. No, wait, I mean to not do yours. Oh, you know what I mean!"

46

"Yes, I do know what you mean," Lisa said coldly, "and it's not exactly fair. I mean, I have to learn a whole new craft! All you have to do—"

"You guys," Carole broke in, "the point is, these resolutions are harder than we expected, right? That's all anyone is saying. Right? You guys?"

There was a stony silence as Stevie and Lisa ate their ice cream. Then Lisa said, more to herself than to anyone, "Maybe what we need is some incentive."

"You mean something to help us keep the resolutions?" Stevie asked. She had been going to suggest that maybe what they needed was to drop the resolutions altogether, A.S.A.P.

Lisa nodded. "Yeah, some reward—no, a penalty for whoever breaks hers first."

"But how will we know if you've broken yours?" Stevie asked pointedly. "You could learn embroidery tomorrow and then have nothing left to do."

Lisa fought against the impulse to toss her ice cream into Stevie's lap. She couldn't remember when she'd last been so irked by a member of The Saddle Club. She wasn't going to try to cheat on her resolution. Why couldn't Stevie just believe that? Probably, Lisa thought cynically, because Stevie was going to cheat on hers—or at least bend it a bit.

47

"Look, I'll vow to embroider every day!" Lisa said exasperatedly. "Would that be satisfactory? Or I'll— I'll—" She floundered, trying to think of something that would convince Stevie that learning embroidery was at least as tough a resolution as being nice to Veronica. After all, Lisa wasn't a lagger! Why, she worked harder than anyone she knew at school. She certainly didn't intend to bring up the rear when it came to these resolutions. "I know," she said, with a sudden inspiration. "I'll vow to embroider something for the bake sale, okay? How about a tablecloth and napkins? We can sell them at the end of the sale."

"That's a great idea, Lisa!" Carole said. "Then your resolution would have a real purpose. You'll make your mom happy and you'll also earn some money for Horse Wise."

Stevie had to agree that Lisa's suggestion was a good one. "All right," she said reluctantly. "That sounds fair."

"Of course, we haven't thought up an incentive yet, so maybe we should just . . ." Lisa let her voice trail off. The resolutions were her idea. So she, of all of them, shouldn't be the one to suggest that they forget about keeping them. Besides, they were a good idea! It would be good for Stevie to lay off

Veronica for a while, it would be good for Carole to eat better food, and, Lisa thought with a sigh, it would be good for her to learn embroidery.

"Maybe we should just what, Lisa?" Stevie challenged her.

"Maybe we should—should think of something really terrible to prevent ourselves from breaking our resolutions," Lisa said in a hurry, trying to keep herself from sounding as defensive as she felt.

"Maybe we should change the subject," Carole said more quietly.

That was all the urging Stevie and Lisa needed. As soon as they switched to a new topic, the girls began to chat amiably. They compared notes on their morning rides, agreed that Mrs. Reg was as loony as ever, and eventually began to discuss the bake sale. Lisa suggested that they spend some time at Pine Hollow going over the Horse Wise equipment to see what they needed. "And I also told my mom that we would make the signs for the bake sale," Lisa said, "and then give them to other members to distribute around Willow Creek."

"Great. We can do that Monday," Carole volunteered.

Stevie said that she thought Lisa's mother would do an excellent job of running the sale.

"If she runs it anything like she runs the PTA Holiday Wreath Sale, Horse Wise is going to rake in the money," Lisa predicted. "I just hope she has enough volunteers."

"Speaking of which, we absolutely must recruit members. We should call every single person who's ever been a part of Horse Wise and make them re-join the club," Carole said.

"I agree," Stevie said, hazel eyes twinkling, "and I think there's one call that Lisa should make."

Lisa burst into laughter. "Just when I thought it was safe to forget all about Simon Atherton, he's back!" she said, mocking an advertisement for a horror movie.

"And if you don't watch out," Carole said menacingly, "he's going to get you!"

The girls found their joke so amusing that they spent the next ten minutes thinking up fake scenarios involving Simon Atherton. "Picture this," Stevie said. "You're at the water fountain, taking a drink. Out of the corner of your eye, you see a pair of feet approaching in sturdy, sensible shoes. You look up—it's him! And he wants to eat lunch with you!"

"No, no, no." Lisa waved her hands. "It's like this: You're at Pine Hollow. It's deserted—or so you

50

think. All of a sudden, behind you, someone says, 'Excuse me, Miss Atwood? Would you do me the honor of discussing tomorrow's algebra assignment on horseback as we wend our way down a local trail?' "

Stevie and Carole snorted with laughter. Lisa could perfectly imitate Simon's formal speech and his upper-class, English way of talking. "I guess for the sake of Horse Wise, though, we have to call him if he's back in town as Mrs. Reg says," Lisa commented.

"Attagirl," said Stevie, toasting water glasses with Lisa. "Do it for the club."

"Me? Who said anything about me?" Lisa joked.

Carole sighed with relief—not because she knew that one of them would relent and call Simon, but because Stevie and Lisa were acting normal toward each other again. Usually Stevie's and Lisa's opposing personalities complemented each other. Even though Lisa got straight As and Stevie barely got by, both girls were smart. Both were funny, too, though their senses of humor were very different. But on the rare occasions that the girls clashed, they clashed hard. Then it fell to Carole to act as the peacemaker between them. When her best friends argued, it was upsetting. She often thought how much simpler it would be if they could just bare their teeth at one another the way horses did. Then everything would be out in the open. There would be no hidden tensions that surfaced all of a sudden.

"What do you think, Carole?" Lisa asked.

Carole focused on Lisa's expectant face. "Huh? What do I think about what?"

"Have you been spacing out again, Carole?" Stevie teased. "Thinking about Starlight's smooth canter again?"

Carole grinned. "Actually, this was one of the few times I was thinking about people and not horses. What did I miss?"

"Stevie has come up with a brilliant idea," Lisa announced.

"For the bake sale? For Horse Wise?" asked Carole.

"Nope. For us," said Lisa. "So we don't break our resolutions."

"What?" asked Carole nervously, afraid that the idea was going to be something that would create more aggravation among the three of them.

Lisa and Stevie twittered for a moment. Then Stevie burst out, "Simon Atherton!"

"Simon Atherton?" said Carole, not comprehending.

"Yes, Simon Atherton," said Lisa. "Whichever one of us breaks our resolution first has to call up Simon and ask him out on a date!"

"A date?" Carole asked. "You mean a real date?"

"Yup, a real date, like going to the movies together," said Stevie.

Lisa and Stevie watched to see how Carole would react. Slowly Carole began to grin. First she grinned a little, then a lot. "I can tell you one thing: I sure as heck am not going to be the one to lose!"

"That's exactly what I said!" Lisa agreed.

"Imagine what Phil would say if I lost!" Stevie wailed. "Imagine if I had to tell him that I was going out for an evening with someone else, and that the someone else was Simon Atherton!"

Lisa and Carole shrieked with delight. Phil Marsten was Stevie's boyfriend. The two had been going out for a while, but it wasn't so serious that if Stevie really wanted to (or in this case, *had* to) go to the movies with another boy she couldn't. Phil would probably be annoyed, but Stevie would make him put up with it. And, as Stevie always said, just because she was going out with Phil didn't mean she couldn't be interested in other boys. Of course, usually when she said that, she didn't have Simon Atherton in mind.

"So, problem solved," Lisa declared.

"Problem solved," Stevie agreed.

Carole took one last sip of her lemonade. She peeled the lid off the cup and looked at the ice in the bottom. She sighed. Right about now she would really have enjoyed a big chocolate chip cone. Instead she slurped up some of the sugary water. "You guys?" she said. "I have a suggestion."

Lisa and Stevie looked up readily.

"Lisa," Carole continued, "maybe you can embroider every day from here until eternity, and Stevie, maybe you'll never be mean to Veronica again, but personally, I need to put a time limit on my resolution, because there's no way I'm giving up junk food for life."

"Hear! Hear!" Stevie said at once.

"Of course there should be a time limit!" Lisa said. "Without a doubt!"

"Oh, good," said Carole, relieved that she had at least partially expressed her opinion. "How about three months?"

"Three months? How about two?" Stevie said.

"Forget two. One month is plenty," Lisa jumped in.

"One month, then?" Carole asked. There was a pause as the three girls looked at one another. Carole had the funny feeling that there was something they weren't saying—that somehow they were still being dishonest with one another.

"You know—" said Stevie.

"We could—" said Lisa.

Both of them broke off abruptly and looked down at their empty dishes.

"I guess I'd better get home," Carole said finally.

"That's what I was going to say," Stevie said right away.

"Me too—got to get home and start that embroidery," Lisa said, doing her best to smile at the prospect. After making a plan to meet at Pine Hollow the following afternoon, the three girls put money down for the check and left—even more quietly than they had come in.

"WHAT THE—?" Lisa sat up in bed, disoriented.

"Are you all right, honey?" Mrs. Atwood knocked on the door and then poked her head in.

"Oh, yeah, Mom." Lisa rubbed her eyes. Scattered over the bed were scissors, needles, thread, and a paperback entitled *Embroidery Made Fun and Easy*. "I was just doing some background reading," Lisa explained hastily.

"All right, I don't want to disturb you. I just wanted to tell you that dinner's in half an hour, so you can set the table in fifteen minutes or so." Mrs. Atwood began to close the door behind her.

"Mom?" Lisa asked, remembering her thoughts before she had fallen asleep. "Do you think the bake sale will be a success?"

"I hope so, Lisa. If I have anything to say about it, it will be. I called a few more mothers and fathers this afternoon, and everyone seems very willing to help. Oh, and I ran into Connie Atherton uptown, and she said that her son is—"

"Connie *who*?" Lisa cried, fully awake at once.

Mrs. Atwood gave Lisa a strange look. "Connie Atherton, sweetheart. You know the Athertons, don't you? I think Simon is about your age. Anyway, they're just back from Texas, and Mrs. Atherton said that Simon is very eager to start riding at Pine Hollow again, so I told her you'd give him a call." Mrs. Atwood beamed at her daughter. "There's a new Horse Wise member right there," she said. "Right?"

As soon as the door closed, Lisa lay back against her pillows and covered her eyes. Here it was, the first of January, and already the year was horrible! For starters, Max's surprise announcement that Horse Wise was in jeopardy. Then her own stupid promise to embroider a whole tablecloth—not to mention a set of napkins—in two weeks. And now the whole world seemed to be conspiring to throw her back together with Simon Atherton. She was *not* going to end up calling him for a date, no matter what. Whoever did lose the bet, Lisa thought wryly, was going to be in for an evening she would never forget.

First of all, to get the conversation going, Simon would probably want to talk about the advanced calculus class he was no doubt taking by now. And forget going to a movie—that was way too normal for Simon. Lisa was sure he'd suggest staying home and looking at the stamp collection he was so proud of.

But there was something else bothering Lisa, too—something that, by comparison, made Simon Atherton seem like a pleasant problem to have. Lisa couldn't quite put her finger on why, but it seemed as if Stevie and Carole were angry at her. But what had she done? Yes, she had suggested the resolutions, but they could have said no or backed out any time. And why should they care, when Lisa's resolution was by far the most difficult? All Carole had to do was say no to chips and dessert; all Stevie had to do was treat Veronica like a normal human being. Yet they'd been acting as if they had agreed to run a marathon! Obviously, they just weren't used to discipline.

Lisa set her lips in a thin line. Let them keep up

their complaining. Lisa, at least, was going to make something of this new year. She was going to get something accomplished and help Horse Wise while she was at it. She'd amaze Stevie, Carole, her mother, Mrs. Reg, Max—everyone—with how fast she'd learn to embroider! Not just to avoid Simon, but to *win*.

Lisa grabbed the embroidery book. She turned to the first page. It had a picture of a smiling woman wearing a turtleneck and jumper. The jumper was embroidered with animals, trees, and flowers in a complicated pattern. "Impress your friends with beautifully embroidered clothing and linens!" read the caption underneath the photograph.

Lisa grinned. She liked the sound of "impress your friends." Humming excitedly, she turned to the index at the back of the book. There was no entry under "tablecloths," but after a minute's searching she found "kitchen and bath linens." Under that heading, the book suggested the fishbone stitch:

Bring the thread through at (A) and make a small straight stitch along the center line of the shape. Bring the thread through again at (B) and make a sloping stitch across the center line at the base of the first stitch. Bring the thread through at (C) and make an overlapping, sloping stitch, which you will alternate with the French knots and previously mastered fly and coral stitches. Then return to point (A) and . . .

Lisa's eyes began to swim. She couldn't concentrate. She had a sudden flashback to a school day the year before. She'd misread her assignment pad and found herself sitting in class, taking a math test that she hadn't studied for. Only the math test had been easier to figure out than these stitches.

CAROLE'S STOMACH GRUMBLED loudly. She hadn't heard her father go into the kitchen, but it had to be almost dinnertime. After getting home from TD's, Carole had eaten a turkey sandwich and an apple, forgoing her usual snack-sized bag of chips. Then, for an afternoon snack, she'd eaten a pear instead of the chocolate bar she would have preferred. Now she was starving. If only her father would—

"Carole! Hungry yet?"

Carole jumped up at the sound of her father's voice. "Coming!" she yelled.

"Grab a coat. We're going out tonight!" Colonel Hanson called.

Even better, Carole thought. At restaurants it was

easy to eat a lot of food that wasn't junk. "Where to, Dad?" she asked, coming downstairs.

"To Willow Creek's finest," Colonel Hanson joked. "Pizza Town!"

Carole's face fell.

"Bundle up, it's cold out," her father said.

As she put on mittens and a scarf, Carole tried to think of a polite way to tell her father that she couldn't eat pizza. Maybe she could just suggest a different place.

In the car on the way over, Carole said, "Are you sure you want to go to Pizza Town, Dad?"

"Yes sirree!" Colonel Hanson answered. "I can taste that pepperoni and sausage now—mmm-mmm. Maybe we should get two mediums instead of one large for more variety. Plus we could have the leftovers tomorrow. What do you think?"

Before Carole could reply, Colonel Hanson rushed on. "Say, we still have to discuss the bake sale, too, don't we? What do you want to make?"

Carole smiled in spite of herself. Colonel Hanson was definitely not one of the parents who needed to be coaxed into putting more time and energy into Horse Wise! "I thought we could make lemon squares," Carole suggested.

"My feelings exactly," Colonel Hanson said seriously. "And I know someone else is bringing chocolate chip cookies, but that doesn't mean we can't make *double*-chocolate chippers, does it?"

Carole laughed at her dad's solemn tone. "No, Dad, I don't think that would be a problem."

"Phew. So, it's decided then. I'll run our choices by Mrs. Atwood as soon as possible. Boy, am I glad that woman is organizing it. Wow, all this talking about food has gotten me hungry. . . . Hey, I've got an idea! Let's get the pizza to go. Then we can stop on the way home and rent a movie. How does that sound?"

"The movie sounds good," Carole said slowly, stalling for time. "But maybe we should go to the vegetarian restaurant and get take-out salads instead." She held her breath to see what her father would say.

"Ha-ha! Good one, Carole!" Colonel Hanson slapped his thigh. "And after that, I'll steam some brown rice and vegetables!"

"But Dad—" Carole stopped. Her suggestion hadn't produced exactly the reaction she'd expected.

Still laughing at what he thought was a joke, Carole's father continued, "For breakfast, we can eat raw carrots! Or some of that hot wheat cereal, right? No more Sugar Pops. And then . . ."

In vain, Carole tried to interrupt as her father went on making fun of "rabbit food." After listening for a few minutes, Carole realized that she should have known better. Other friends' parents had been hit by the health kick, but not her father. His idea of a healthy meal was ordering fried chicken instead of fried steak! Since her mother had died, Carole had pretty much gone along with her father's eating habits. But now, with the New Year's resolution, it was time to make a few changes.

"Dad," Carole said, in a clear, firm voice.

"Don't worry, honey—I haven't forgotten the movie snacks! We'll pick up some chocolate-covered raisins and microwave popcorn and Jujyfruits, too."

Carole studied her father's profile. He looked as excited as a little boy. She couldn't wreck his plan with her silly resolution! Why had she ever let Lisa talk her into it in the first place? It was easy for Lisa. All she had to do was pick up a needle and thread for half an hour, not change her whole diet!

"It's your last night of vacation. Might as well make it a classic Hanson movie night, huh?"

"That would be great, Dad, but listen, I have something to ask you."

"Yes?"

Tell him, Carole said to herself. *No more junk food!* "Can we make one of the pizzas mushroom and pepper?" she asked instead. How sinful could a vegetarian pizza be?

Colonel Hanson grinned. "Great. That ought to balance the pepperoni and sausage. Say, do you want to invite Stevie to join us?"

Carole was surprised at how emphatically she shook her head. "No thanks, Dad. I think it would be nice to keep it just the two of us." The last thing Carole wanted was a member of The Saddle Club checking up on her! And after their conversation at TD's, Carole had seen—and heard—quite enough of Stevie and Lisa for the day.

Colonel Hanson pulled into the parking lot of Pizza Town. "You know what? You're right. And with only two of us, there'll be more junk food!"

STEVIE GRABBED THE PLASTIC bottle of bubble bath, opened it, and poured a long stream of pink liquid into the running tap water. Despite the less-than-thrilling morning, Stevie was in a good mood. First of all, she had a week more of vacation. Fenton Hall was a private school. The school day at Fenton was longer, but so were the Christmas breaks and summer vacations. Knowing that Lisa and Carole had to go back the next day made Stevie appreciate her own last week even more. She would miss them at Pine Hollow during the day, but she wouldn't miss homework and getting up at six-thirty!

Thinking of The Saddle Club made Stevie giggle. Every time she pictured Lisa or Carole calling up Simon Atherton to ask him out on a date, she cracked up. Because, of course, one of them was going to lose the bet. Meanwhile Stevie had thought up a perfect way to keep her own resolution. In answer to everything Veronica said, Stevie was going to smile and say, "That's nice, Veronica."

Stepping gingerly into her hot bath, Stevie giggled again. "That's nice, Veronica," she said aloud, practicing her line.

" 'My lesson with Johannes was incredible,' " Stevie mimicked.

"That's nice, Veronica."

" 'I'm the biggest snob in Pine Hollow.' "

"That's nice, Veronica. Ha-ha-ha!"

Still chuckling, Stevie settled into the bath and let the bubbles close over her. There was another reason she knew she was going to win: When it came to games or contests of any kind, she had a ruthless competitive streak. Usually she focused it on Veronica, riders from rival Pony Clubs, or her three brothers. But, Stevie thought slyly, there was no reason why she couldn't put it to use against The Saddle Club. Or not exactly *against*— that sounded too hostile. But there was no reason she couldn't use her competitive edge to win the bet.

As for Horse Wise, Stevie was sure the bake sale would make a lot of money. The main thing for The Saddle Club to worry about was getting new members—or getting old members like Simon Atherton to rejoin. Stevie snickered. Maybe she would call Simon personally to get the ball rolling. She could even butter him up a little—drop hints that Carole and Lisa really wanted to be friends with him again, now that he was back.

"Stevie, are you in there? Hurry up!" Stevie's twin brother, Alex, banged on the bathroom door.

"Hold your horses!" Stevie yelled. "I'm taking a bath, and I'm not getting out anytime soon!"

"You'd better get out soon!" Alex yelled.

"Or what?" Stevie demanded.

"Or—or else!" Alex replied.

In response, Stevie stood up in the tub, reached over, and locked the bathroom door.

"Mom!" Alex screamed.

Stevie grinned delightedly. So far, this new year was starting out just fine.

6

"THIS IS THE WORST new year ever!" Stevie cried. She was sitting at breakfast the next morning with her mother, father, and three brothers.

"Tell that to Miss Fenton," Stevie's mother said flatly.

"That's right, Stevie, tell that to Miss Fenton," Alex repeated.

"Alex," Mr. Lake said warningly, "why don't you, Chad, and Michael excuse us. This is between your sister and us."

Grumbling a bit, the boys stood up with their empty cereal bowls and left the table.

"I just don't understand why you didn't tell me before!" Stevie wailed when they had gone.

"Miss Fenton only called last night, Stevie," said Mrs. Lake. "And to tell you the truth, I think it's awfully nice of the teacher to let you retake the test."

"Nice!" Stevie scoffed. "More like torture! How can I study this week? It's my last week of vacation!"

"You'll find a way," Mr. Lake predicted. "I'll quiz you tonight on your vocabulary."

"All of it? But that's—"

"Case closed," Mrs. Lake said. "Now try to have a good day."

"Yeah, right," Stevie muttered, staring miserably into her mug of hot chocolate. Overnight, her new year had gone from marvelous to horrible. Her parents had received a call from the headmistress of her school. Winter term was half over, and Stevie had done so badly on the French midterm exam that her teacher wanted her to retake it. The retake would be in a week's time—the first day back. That meant that instead of just hanging out at Pine Hollow, Stevie would have to spend part of the week studying for it.

"Oh, Stevie, I almost forgot," Mrs. Lake said, returning momentarily to the table. "Miss Fenton said that there's another girl who's going to retake the test—Veronica diAngelo. Maybe you two could study together."

Stevie stared at her mother as if she were a creature from outer space. "I'd rather walk on hot coals for the next ten years!" she cried.

As soon as her parents left for work, Stevie got out her French book, shoved it into her backpack, and hightailed it over to Pine Hollow. French could wait. For now, she had her mental state to consider. And the only thing she could think of that would cheer her up was a nice, long ride on Belle. She groomed the mare quickly, eager to set off on one of the trails. The winters in Willow Creek were fairly mild, so even in January it was still possible to ride outside. The other bonus to riding outside was that Veronica diAngelo hardly ever went trail riding in the winter. She liked to stay warm in the indoor ring.

"Stevie! Hey, Stevie!"

At the sound of the high-pitched voice, Stevie cringed. With an effort, she managed to keep her voice pleasant, as the other girl caught up to her in the aisle. "Hello, Veronica."

"Hey, Stevie. I'm glad I ran into you. My mother

told me you had to retake the French test, too," Veronica said.

"That's nice, Veronica," Stevie replied. Veronica ignored her.

"I'd offer to study with you—"

"That's nice, Veronica," Stevie said, surprised that it was almost true.

"—but since I have my own private tutor, it just wouldn't be helpful to me to hear all of your errors."

Stevie bit her lip hard. "That's nice, Veronica," she said through clenched teeth. Her surefire plan wasn't as easy to stick to as she had hoped. It was almost causing her physical pain not to retort to Veronica's rude comments. Veronica followed her into the tack room.

"You're probably dying to hear how my lesson with Johannes was. Okay, I won't keep you in suspense: It was amazing! He thinks I have real talent," Veronica bragged.

"How much did you pay him to say that?" Stevie muttered.

"What?"

"I said, that's nice, Veronica," Stevie replied.

"Johannes thinks that Danny and I are headed for the Olympics," Veronica gushed.

"Yeah, when pigs fly," Stevie muttered. Danny,

Veronica's expensive show horse, might actually have had a shot at the Olympics, but with a different rider—a rider far superior to Veronica.

"What was that?" Veronica looked at Stevie curiously.

Stevie thought about sticking her tongue out at Veronica or pulling her hair. Then she remembered Simon Atherton. Even the idea of sitting next to him in a dark movie theater made her stomach turn. Stevie cleared her throat. "I said, that's nice Veronica. Very, very nice. Very, very, very, very, very, very nice. Got it? It's nice, okay?"

"Okay, okay, jeez—you don't have to yell," Veronica said.

Stevie grabbed her hard hat and stuck it on her head, hurrying so she could escape to the trail.

"Do you really have time to ride?" Veronica asked. "Shouldn't you be home studying for the test?"

"Shouldn't you?" Stevie shot back. She cursed herself for letting Veronica get a rise out of her.

"Me? No, I've got plenty of time to ride. My tutor is going to have me ready in no time. I'll bet you're dying to know who's tutoring me, aren't you, Stevie?" Veronica prompted.

"No, I'm not," Stevie snapped. Just because she had resolved to be nice to Veronica didn't mean that she had to be extra polite, did it?

"Fine. But when I get an A on the retest, you'll be sorry!" Veronica chanted in a singsong.

Stevie forced herself to take a deep breath and count to ten. "That's nice, Veronica," she repeated mechanically. As Veronica chattered away, Stevie did her best to block out the noise. So far, Stevie realized, her plan to annoy Veronica was utterly failing. Veronica hadn't even noticed that she was repeating the same sentence!

"What did you say?" Veronica asked sharply.

Stevie snapped back to attention. "I said that it was nice."

"That what was nice?" Veronica demanded.

"Whatever you said," Stevie said, smiling. This was more like it.

"But I don't understand. I just said that it's too bad Belle could never be the jumper that Danny is. Otherwise you could take lessons with Johannes Wendt, too."

Stevie beamed. "That's nice, Veronica."

"Is that all you're going to say?" Veronica demanded. " 'That's nice'?"

"Yup."

"But why should you think it's nice? You sound like a broken record."

"That's nice, Veronica."

"A horrible, scratched, annoying broken record—"

"That's nice, Veronica."

"—that ought to be thrown in the trash!" Veronica shrieked.

Stevie didn't respond. Instead she hunted through the tack room clutter to find her crop. She was so distracted by not being mean to Veronica that she almost didn't notice what a mess the tack room was. Saddles were hung up every which way, reins and parts of bridles lay on the floor, and there was a pile of bandages that needed rolling.

"What day is today, Veronica?" Stevie asked suddenly.

"It's Monday. Why? Do you have a date? Ha, ha."

"Monday? Oh, great. Red O'Malley leads a beginner Horse Wise unmounted session in here on Monday afternoons," Stevie said almost to herself. Red O'Malley was Max's head stable hand. A wonderful rider himself, Red preferred exercising horses, teaching, and barn work to competing in shows. He was truly Max's right-hand man.

"So what if there's a meeting here?" Veronica demanded.

"So look at the place!" Stevie exclaimed. "It's a complete mess. If Max sees this, he'll want to forget about the trial period and end Horse Wise today!"

Veronica's expression changed from smugness to shock. "End Horse Wise? What are you talking about?"

Stevie looked at Veronica. It seemed impossible, but Veronica actually seemed serious. "You mean you don't know?"

"Know what?" Veronica demanded. "Stevie, tell me!"

"At the meeting yesterday, which you missed, Max put Horse Wise on trial. We have to prove to him that we're dedicated to keeping the club going. Otherwise, he might put an end to the club. We need more members, and more money, too. That's why we're having the big bake sale." At Veronica's inquiring look, Stevie explained about Mrs. Atwood's idea for the bake sale. She could hardly believe that she was having a normal conversation with Veronica. But despite Veronica's lack of interest in most of Horse Wise, she seemed genuinely concerned about Max's threat to put an end to the club. "Anyway, the sale is on Saturday in two weeks, at the shopping center," Stevie concluded. "Lisa is going to embroider a tablecloth and napkins to raffle off at the end of the sale."

"A bake sale?" Veronica sneered. All at once she sounded like her true, snobby self again. "Embroidery? Isn't that kind of small-town?"

Stevie was about to turn away, disgusted, but something—Horse Wise, her resolution—made her try again. "We *live* in a small town, in case you've forgotten. And it would be great if you could help. We need every last person if we're going to keep this club alive."

With that, Stevie picked up the nearest saddle and replaced it neatly on its rack. She could feel Veronica's eyes on her as she began to clean up the tack room. It was almost as if Veronica wanted to help but didn't know how. Strangely enough, Stevie didn't feel as annoyed by her as she usually did.

"Stevie?" Veronica said. "I've got to go meet a friend for a ride now, and I don't know how to bake anything, but I'll talk to my father. He could donate something to raffle off—something really good, not just some embroidered tablecloth. Hey, I know: a helicopter ride over the city like the one I took on New Year's Eve."

Stevie paused in the middle of rolling a bandage. In the space of about ten seconds, Veronica had managed to be rude and thoughtless as well as polite and generous. Stevie hardly knew how to respond. Then she thought of the perfect answer. She grinned and said, "That's nice, Veronica. Very nice."

WHISTLING, CAROLE JOINED the hot-lunch line in the cafeteria. It was always a relief when the morning was over and it was time for lunch period—especially when she spotted Lisa, as she did just then. Lisa had finished loading her tray and was heading toward an empty table. "I'll save you a seat!" she called when Carole got her attention.

"Great!" Carole called back. Because Lisa was in a grade higher than Carole, the two girls had different groups of friends. But Lisa's lunch period had recently been switched to the same time as Carole's, so now they liked to eat together when they could. The Saddle Club was a stronger bond than Willow Creek Junior High, after all.

"Boy, am I glad this day is half over," Carole said, sitting down next to Lisa.

"Tell me about it. All my teachers are piling on

extra work. It's like they want to make up for the free time we had over vacation," Lisa commented. "And my mom had me up early this morning to help her make calls about the bake sale."

"Oh, I'm supposed to tell you that we're bringing lemon squares and double-chocolate chippers," Carole said, giggling. "My dad is planning an all-day bake-a-thon."

"The next two weeks are going to feel like a bake-a-thon to me," said Lisa. "My mom is going crazy organizing it."

"How's the embroidery going?" Carole asked, picking up half a hamburger. The minute she asked it, Carole wanted to take the question back. She and Lisa had been having a nice, friendly talk. Why did she have to go and bring up the subject of resolutions?

Lisa fiddled with her napkin. "It's going fine," she said briefly. "Just fine. How's not eating junk food going?"

Carole finished chewing her bite and swallowed. Was it her imagination or was Lisa staring at her hamburger? Maybe a hamburger wasn't the best thing in the world, but what else was she supposed to eat? The other choice for hot lunch was macaroni and cheese! Was that less "junky" than a hamburger? "I guess it's going fine," Carole said tentatively. "Do you think—I mean, should I— Look, am I breaking my resolution by eating a hamburger?"

"Carole!" Lisa protested. "I'm not here to tell you what you can't eat."

But despite what Lisa said, Carole was sure that she disapproved of the hamburger. All of a sudden, the hamburger didn't taste very good. Carole put it down on her plate.

"What's wrong?" Lisa asked.

"I don't know. I'm just not that hungry anymore," Carole lied. Actually she was starved. She had been looking forward to lunch practically since breakfast, but she certainly didn't intend to eat while Lisa watched.

The two girls shifted uncomfortably in their seats and picked at their food for a few minutes. Around them, the cafeteria resounded with lunchtime din.

"You know, I should—"

"I think I'll—"

"You first," said Lisa.

"No, you," Carole said.

"I was just thinking that I should probably get

back to the classroom early. I want to look over my math assignment," Lisa said.

"Okay, then I'll see you this afternoon at Pine Hollow," Carole said quickly.

Lisa stood up. "Right. See you at Pine Hollow."

"Say," Carole called, trying to bring a touch of humor into the situation, "is Simon Atherton in your math class?"

Lisa half smiled as she shook her head. "No, I guess he's moved even farther ahead of the rest of us." She hesitated a moment and then added, "You know, it's funny, but I've mentioned him to a few kids and nobody seems to know who I'm talking about."

Carole nodded thoughtfully. "That is funny. He's so hard to miss: tall, skinny as a rail, tufts of blond hair sticking out in all directions . . ."

Lisa laughed. "Glasses as thick as Coke bottles. I can't believe we haven't spotted him yet."

"Say, Lisa, maybe you ought to stay and finish lunch with me. Otherwise, Simon might appear and ask if he can sit here," Carole pointed out.

Lisa was glad of the excuse to stay. She pulled out her chair and sat down again. She didn't really have to get to her classroom early; she just didn't want Carole to think she was checking up on her. Lisa was beginning to think that maybe Carole did have the hardest resolution. These days it was impossible to tell what was junk food and what was health food, especially in the cafeteria of Willow Creek Junior High.

7

By the time Stevie finished cleaning up the tack room, it was early afternoon. Lisa and Carole would be arriving in an hour or so to start making an inventory of Horse Wise equipment. The girls were also planning to make signs for the bake sale for members to post around Willow Creek. More than anything, Stevie was dying to tack up Belle and go for a quick ride. But if she rode now, she'd have to leave Pine Hollow early to go home and study her French vocabulary. Her father would expect her to know at least some of it by dinnertime. So Stevie did the only sensible thing. She got her book from her backpack, found an out-of-the-way bale of hay, sat down, and started to study. Every so often she looked over her shoulder. If she saw anyone coming she would slam her book shut and hide it. It would never do to have people saying that Stevie Lake was becoming a bookworm. She'd lost enough credibility already by being nice to Veronica!

The bale of hay Stevie had chosen was opposite Patch's stall. The old pinto stuck his nose out to greet her. "Don't bother me, boy," Stevie said, her eyes on the page.

Patch pricked up his ears.

"I know," Stevie muttered. "This is the craziest thing I've ever done. Studying on my own initiative. I must be sick or something."

At the sound of Stevie's voice, Patch's neighbor poked his head out, too. Out of the corner of her eye, Stevie saw a pretty chestnut face with a long, broad blaze. Forgetting her *français* for a second, Stevie looked up. "Hey, boy. Wow, you *are* pretty. Mrs. Reg was right." Stevie studied the gelding's face. It was hard to believe the horse had been a gangly yearling colt with a head that looked too big for his body. Now he was an attractive, bright chestnut gelding, well on the way to maturity.

"What did I tell you? Pretty, huh?"

Stevie started. "Oh, it's only you, Mrs. Reg," she said, relieved, as the older woman came around the corner.

"Only me?" said Mrs. Reg.

"I mean, I'm *glad* it's you," Stevie corrected herself. "I don't want anyone else to catch me studying. They'll think I've become a nerd!"

"Nerds are people, too," Mrs. Reg chided her. "You know, Stevie, some of the best people I know started out as nerds."

"Sure, Mrs. Reg. I agree," Stevie said, hoping to stop Max's mother before she got going.

Luckily Mrs. Reg seemed distracted. "Have you seen Veronica?" she asked.

Stevie nodded. "I think she went riding with a friend."

"Well, if you see her, tell her I'm looking for her. I want to thank her."

"Thank her for what?" Stevie asked suspiciously.

"You're not going to believe this," Mrs. Reg said, leaning in confidentially, "but I think Veronica has turned over a new leaf for the new year. The tack room was a mess this morning, a real mess, and she—"

"She cleaned it up?" Stevie gasped, her face white with anger.

"Yes, how did you know?" Mrs. Reg asked.

"If you don't mind my asking, how did *you* know, Mrs. Reg?" Stevie inquired, her voice shaking.

"Veronica let it slip herself. But she's being very modest about it. She doesn't want anyone to know," Mrs. Reg whispered. "So let's keep it between us, okay?"

Stevie nodded as Mrs. Reg disappeared down the aisle. She was so boiling mad she didn't trust herself to speak. How could she have let down her guard around Veronica for one minute? It never failed! The minute Veronica did even one little thing that seemed halfway decent, like saying she would talk to her father about making a donation for Horse Wise, she went and did some huge, awful thing that reversed everything—like lying to Mrs. Reg about cleaning the tack room!

Stevie was burning to tell Mrs. Reg the truth, but she hated tattletales almost as much as she hated Veronica. Anyway, it might just look as if she was sour at Veronica. Normally Stevie would have found a way to get back at the girl and make her fess up, but, thanks to her stupid resolution, her hands were tied.

For a few minutes, Stevie tried to concentrate on her studying. Instead of French nouns and adjectives though, she kept seeing pictures of Veronica—pictures she felt like throwing darts at or ripping into a million pieces! If only Lisa and Carole would show up. They'd know what to do. The minute the thought ran through her head, she heard a familiar voice.

"If only we could find Stevie, then—" Lisa was saying as she and Carole walked down the aisle.

"Hey! Lisa. Carole. I was just wishing that you guys would show up," Stevie exclaimed.

"We both came right from school, so we got here fifteen minutes ago," said Carole. "Hey, is that a textbook in your hand?"

"Oh, this? Oh, um, not really. I just found it here. Simon Atherton must have been doing a little extra homework—" Stevie stopped when she saw the doubtful looks her friends were giving her. "Okay! Okay! You caught me. I'm failing French so I have to retake a test in a week."

Carole and Lisa burst out laughing. Other kids worried about not studying enough. Stevie worried about being "caught" studying at all. *"Je t'aiderai,"* Lisa said promptly.

"Huh?" Stevie asked.

"I'll help you," Lisa translated, grinning.

"Oh, right—help—*aider*—I knew that," Stevie

said. "That would be good. That would be *très, très bien!* How about on the phone this evening?" Stevie asked, thinking of Veronica's private tutor. Two could play that game, and Lisa was the best tutor Stevie had ever had.

"Sure, anytime, Stevie," Lisa replied. "But for now let's hit the locker room."

Next to the locker room was a closet where Max stored show equipment over the winter. As the three of them headed there, Stevie filled Lisa and Carole in on Veronica's latest. She tried to keep her voice down, but it was extremely difficult. What she wanted to do was scream until she was blue in the face: "Veronica diAngelo is a huge liar!"

"The thing that gets me," said Lisa, "is that Veronica probably thought she could get away with it. If Mrs. Reg hadn't said anything to you, you never would have known that Veronica took the credit."

"I know. I'm ready to throttle her," Stevie said angrily. She stole a quick glance at the other two. "I mean, not that I would actually *do* anything or—or even say anything for that matter," she added hastily.

Lisa and Carole rushed to reassure Stevie that they knew what she meant. Privately Lisa thought that Stevie deserved to say or do whatever she felt like to Veronica. But she couldn't very well admit that. It would be like giving Stevie permission to break her resolution. How could Stevie be the loser of the bet if Lisa encouraged her to lose? For the second time that day, Lisa found herself not being able to say what she felt like saying to one of her best friends.

"Boy, is this place a pit," Carole observed. They had opened the closet and were looking in.

"Yeah, it looks just like the tack room before Veronica cleaned it up," Stevie said sarcastically.

"Gosh, I can really understand what Max was talking about," said Lisa. "Nobody's been in here for months." The closet was crammed full of Pony Club equipment: buckets, brushes, tools, spare tack, riding clothes, study manuals, hay nets, and more. Lisa took one more look. "Okay, let's get to work."

In no time at all, Lisa had Stevie and Carole hauling out the stuff and organizing it into piles. Meanwhile Lisa cataloged each item, making a note as to what kind of condition the item was in. She formed three categories: excellent, acceptable, and "If we don't get a new one, we're going to fail every stable management test we take."

Unlike horse shows, Pony Club events tested competitors not only on riding skills but also on horsemanship. Judges walked around the teams' stabling areas to inspect them for safety and efficiency. A bad stable management score could—and often did—mean the difference between winning and coming home from an event empty-handed.

Under Max's strict coaching, Horse Wise had always prided itself on near-perfect stable management scores. Looking at the growing list of "If we don't get a new one . . ." items, Lisa had to wonder how Max had kept things together for so long. Buckets had rusty handles; hay nets were torn. There was a whole pile of laundry from the past season that had never been washed: It was impossible to tell if the grass and manure stains on the leg bandages would come out. But despite the huge amount of work that needed to be done (and the money that had to be raised), Lisa found that she was enjoying the effort. It was a relief to work alongside Stevie and Carole, as they usually did, instead of feeling that the three of them were in competition with one another. Sorting through the stuff made the girls remember old times, too.

"Remember at our first rally when Stevie went to inspection with these on her feet?" Carole asked, with a grin. She held up a pair of protective boot rubbers.

Stevie howled. "Yeah, I was standing there ready to present Topside to the judge. We'd been up all night polishing tack until it was cleaner than the day we bought it, my boots were glowing in the dark, and I'd forgotten to take off the galoshes!"

Lisa started to giggle. "I was signaling you like crazy and then the judge turned around and caught me!"

"Luckily he gave us a couple of points for team effort, didn't he?" Carole asked.

"Yup. I talked him into it," Stevie said. "I have no idea how, but I talked him into it."

The girls reminisced some more, and before they knew it the closet was completely neat and reorganized. Hearing Mrs. Reg whistling in the aisle outside, they called her in to see.

"I come bearing gifts," Mrs. Reg announced after she had oohed and aahed over the closet. She held up a plastic bowl and took off the lid. Inside was an assortment of freshly baked cookies. "These are a few recipes I'm trying for the bake sale. I need them taste-tested. Will you girls do the honors?"

"And how!" Stevie cried, grabbing a handful.

"We'd love to, Mrs. Reg," Lisa said politely. She peered into the bowl and selected a coconut drop and a ginger snap.

"Carole, how about you? Don't be shy," Mrs. Reg urged.

Carole pursed her lips. The cookies looked utterly delicious. She was very hungry. She looked up at Mrs. Reg. "Are any of those health cookies, Mrs. Reg?" Carole asked.

"No, but a little sugar won't hurt you, Carole. Dig in," said Mrs. Reg.

"I can't," Carole said reluctantly.

Stevie and Lisa exchanged guilty looks. They felt horrible watching Carole say no to Mrs. Reg's home-baked cookies. But what could they do?

Mrs. Reg looked hard at the three of them. "Is something going on here? Why can't Carole have a cookie?"

"It's not them, Mrs. Reg," Carole hastened to explain. "It's me. It was my New Year's resolution."

"What was?" Mrs. Reg asked. "Not to eat cookies?"

"No. Not to eat junk food," Carole said.

"Junk food?" Mrs. Reg said. "My cookies aren't junk! They've got oatmeal and sugar and butter and eggs and raisins and coconut in them! All natural ingredients! Junk food is potato chips! And packaged cheese curls! You're not breaking your resolution if you eat one of my cookies. A cookie is just a nice, sweet treat for a nice, sweet girl. Now dig in," Mrs. Reg commanded.

"That's right, dig in!" Stevie said.

"Absolutely," Lisa added. "Take a whole handful."

Carole didn't need to be told again. She took the biggest cookie in the bowl, an oatmeal-raisin, and chomped down on it. If Mrs. Reg said it wasn't junk food, and Lisa and Stevie gave the go-ahead, she wasn't about to say no.

"Now, what's this about New Year's resolutions?" Mrs. Reg asked when they were all chewing contentedly.

"We all made them," Lisa explained, "to make our New Year's Eve more . . . fun."

"Hmm. So, Carole, yours is to stop eating junk food. What's yours, Stevie?"

Stevie smiled sheepishly. "Oh, mine is, um, to be nice to—um, well—just to be nice."

"I see," Mrs. Reg said, with a look that showed that she knew exactly what Stevie wasn't telling her. "Lisa?"

"Mine is to learn embroidery," Lisa mumbled, hoping Mrs. Reg wouldn't ask her if she liked it.

"That sounds like a good one," Mrs. Reg commented. "I've always loved embroidering."

"You have?" Lisa said. "Do you think you could help me learn? I got the book out over the weekend and I couldn't understand one word!"

Now it was Carole and Stevie's turn to exchange looks. That didn't sound like Lisa at all! Usually Lisa mastered a task the minute she set her mind to it. Could it be that she was having trouble sticking to her resolution, too?

"I'd love to help you, Lisa. I've got to start the feeding in an hour, but if you want to come in now, I can start you on a sampler right away," Mrs. Reg said. Mrs. Reg's house was on the Pine Hollow property, about a two-minute walk from the stables.

"You will? That would be great! Oh, but wait," Lisa said, remembering, "we're supposed to make the signs for the bake sale."

"That's okay, Lis'. We're not going to put them up for a week, anyway," Carole said. The girls had decided that it would be best to wait to poster until a couple of days before the sale. That way people would see them and decide to go on the spur of the moment.

"Carole and I can take care of them," Stevie agreed. "It's the least we can do, since you're embroidering a whole tablecloth and napkin set for the sale."

Lisa grimaced. Why did Stevie have to remind her of that rash promise? It was especially inconsiderate when she'd been so sympathetic to Stevie about Veronica. The new year was only a couple of days old, but never in their history could Lisa remember The Saddle Club having so many ups and downs in so short a period.

"A tablecloth and napkin set?" said Mrs. Reg. "Gosh, we've got our work cut out for us, Lisa."

"We sure do," Lisa said. And lately, she thought grimly, she had her work cut out for her staying on good terms with The Saddle Club.

"WHAT DO YOU TAKE in your tea?" Mrs. Reg asked from the kitchen.

"Milk and sugar," Lisa called. A moment later Mrs. Reg appeared, carrying a tray with a teapot, cups, spoons, napkins, a small pitcher, and a bowl of sugar on it.

"I always like a nice, hot cup of tea on a winter afternoon," said the older woman. She set the tray down on the living room coffee table and sat down beside Lisa.

Lisa gratefully accepted the cup Mrs. Reg handed

her. The hot liquid was soothing, and right now Lisa definitely needed her nerves soothed.

"So, let me get this straight: You volunteered to embroider a tablecloth for the bake sale?" Mrs. Reg inquired, stirring milk into her tea.

Lisa nodded. "And napkins. And I know it's going to be hard," she added.

"It is going to be hard. Impossible, in fact," Mrs. Reg confirmed. "Why don't you just do a nice sampler pattern and give it to your mother as a gift? Bake something for the sale if you want to help Horse Wise."

"I could, but I—I don't want to look bad in front of Carole and Stevie," Lisa blurted out. Something about Mrs. Reg's motherly manner always seemed to make Lisa confess her fears.

"Look bad? Oh, you mean the resolutions? But that's silly, Lisa. Friends aren't people you have to worry about looking bad in front of. Friends want what's best for you," Mrs. Reg said, her voice serious.

Lisa frowned. Mrs. Reg had just struck a chord that reverberated in her private thoughts. "That's what I think, too. That's why I wanted to help Stevie and Carole! Carole said she eats too much junk food because her dad is always making snacks when they watch movies. So I told her she should give it up. And Stevie's always getting upset because she has fights with Veronica. So I thought if she resolved to be nice to Veronica, they would stop having fights. But now Veronica is up to her usual tricks, and Carole's always hungry, and I've got to embroider a tablecloth and napkins in less than two weeks!"

Mrs. Reg took a long sip of tea. "You know, Lisa," she said thoughtfully, "when Max was growing up, he told me he wanted to learn to play the piano. So I gave him lessons and made sure he practiced every day—scales, easy classical pieces, all the right things. At first he liked it, but then he started to skip lessons and fool around during his practice hour because he wanted to be in the barn with the horses. So I canceled the lessons, and he quit playing. But a few years later, I started to hear him tinkering on the piano in the evenings. Pretty soon he'd taken it up again. He taught himself all kinds of songs—not classical songs, but popular music, the kind of music he liked to listen to on the radio. That's what he really wanted to play all along. And he got pretty good. He still plays sometimes, but if

I'd made him stick with the classical lessons—wait a minute. What was that about Veronica's 'usual tricks'?"

Startled by the sudden change of subject, Lisa chewed her lip, wondering whether or not she should say something. Then she had an idea: She would try the indirect approach Mrs. Reg herself used. "Mrs. Reg, you know how someone can say something to someone about doing something that the someone didn't really do? Well, you see, sometimes Veronica is that someone."

"I see," Mrs. Reg said gravely. "I see, indeed. Humph."

Lisa waited to see what Mrs. Reg would do. Maybe she shouldn't have said anything at all, but it seemed so unfair to Stevie! Instead of making any comment about Veronica, Mrs. Reg leaned down and took out a bag. "Let's get to work, shall we?"

"Sure, Mrs. Reg," said Lisa, relieved.

From the bag Mrs. Reg took out colored thread, needles, patterns, and fabric. The last item was a curious-looking, round, wooden contraption. "This is an embroidery hoop, dear, the same one my mother learned on and the same one she taught me on."

Lisa took the hoop gingerly in her hands. It gave

her a strange thrill to hold it, knowing it was old and had been used by Mrs. Reg's mother decades ago.

"Now, let's see . . . here we are. A simple sample pattern for you to start with." Mrs. Reg held up a large, square piece of light-colored linen. The letters of the alphabet, encircled by a flower border, were drawn on the linen.

Lisa watched intently as Mrs. Reg took a small needle and threaded it. "What kind of yarn is that?" she asked. With Mrs. Reg beside her, she felt confident again. How hard could this embroidery stuff be?

"It's not yarn, dear. It's called embroidery floss. All right, now—"

"Now we'll start with some French knots, fishbone, and coral stitches, right? And after I'm warmed up can I start right in on the tablecloth?" Lisa inquired eagerly.

Mrs. Reg sat back on the sofa. She smiled. "We'll start with the basic cross-stitch," she said kindly. "If you find it too much of a bore, you can switch, all right?"

"All right," Lisa said, dying to try her hand at the sampler.

Just then the doorbell rang. A puzzled look

crossed Mrs. Reg's face. "Now who could—oh, I re-member. It's the Atherton boy. He's here to do a little yard work for me. Such a sweet boy. And so generous with his time. Have you called him yet about the Horse Wise sale?"

"N-no, but listen, Mrs. Reg, I have to go to the bathroom very badly. Will you excuse me?" Before Mrs. Reg could object, Lisa got up and fled the room. She dashed down the hall into the bathroom and closed the door, panting. What a close escape! In another minute or two, Mrs. Reg would have invited Simon in to join them. Then Lisa would have had to sit there making conversation with him all afternoon instead of working on her embroidery.

Lisa listened to Mrs. Reg thanking Simon. She waited until she heard the front door close. Then she opened the bathroom door and went back to the living room. As she sat down to rejoin Mrs. Reg, she glanced out the window and saw the back of a blond head vanish around the corner of the house.

"I told Simon that one of you girls will be calling him about the bake sale," Mrs. Reg informed Lisa. "So don't waste too much time, because he's eager to help. Simon Atherton is just the kind of person we want in this Pony Club, don't you think?"

"Sure, Mrs. Reg," Lisa replied, stifling a grin, "whatever you say."

AN HOUR LATER, the last thing Lisa felt like doing was smiling. Even with Mrs. Reg's help, embroidery was one of the most frustrating tasks she had attempted. She kept messing up and having to start over. The back of the sampler looked like a war zone, it had so many mistakes.

"I'm horrible at this, Mrs. Reg!" Lisa wailed in exasperation.

"You're not horrible," Mrs. Reg reprimanded her. "You're just a beginner. You're getting all worked up because you're in such a hurry to learn. You've got to take your time, Lisa. Do a little every day."

"But what about the tablecloth?" Lisa said miserably.

"Forget the tablecloth! You can't embroider a whole tablecloth in two weeks! Even I couldn't do that, and I've been embroidering for fifty years!"

Lisa put the sampler down on the table and rested her head in her hands. "I don't know what to do, Mrs. Reg," she admitted.

"I know what you should do now: Go home and eat a good dinner, do your homework, and go to bed early," Mrs. Reg said sternly. "I've got to feed the horses, and you've done enough for now."

Reluctantly, Lisa allowed herself to be talked into quitting for the day. She thanked Mrs. Reg for her help and headed out.

"Don't forget to call Simon about the sale!" Mrs. Reg called as she left.

"I won't!" Lisa promised. To herself she added, *I'll probably have to ask him out on a date while I'm at it!*

"DON'T YOU WANT some popcorn while you do your homework?" Colonel Hanson asked.

"No, thanks, Dad. Dinner was great, and I'm really full," Carole said truthfully. As they often did, she and her father had cooked dinner together— baked chicken and, at Carole's suggestion, a big salad. Carole felt a little bad about saying no to the popcorn, but she knew she was being silly: If she didn't want it, she didn't want it. She shouldn't say yes just to please her father.

"Okeydoke, then I'm only going to pop half a cup for myself," Colonel Hanson said.

"Enjoy it, Dad," Carole said, heading upstairs.

"Will do, honey."

Up in her room Carole had a realization: She had told her father no, and he hadn't minded one bit.

Maybe it was that simple. Maybe she just had to be clear about what she wanted and what she didn't want. And maybe, Carole thought for the first time, these resolutions were a good idea, after all.

Carole had barely started her math homework when the phone rang. It was Stevie. Lisa had been helping her with her French over the phone. "But my brain is so crammed with *le*, *la*, and *les* that I can't learn another word!" Stevie said. "So I thought I'd call and bother you instead."

"Shouldn't we conference in Lisa?" Carole asked.

"Can't. She's got tons of homework plus embroidery homework," Stevie explained.

"Mrs. Reg gave her embroidery homework?" Carole asked.

"No, but you know Lisa," said Stevie. "She wants to work on what Mrs. Reg taught her today."

"So the lesson went well?"

"I guess so. Lisa didn't give me too many of the details—except for one important one, that is! She barely escaped seeing Simon Atherton. He was at Mrs. Reg's to do some yard work. Lisa had to hide in the bathroom so she wouldn't have to talk to him!"

Picturing Lisa running into the bathroom brought a smile to Carole's lips, but then she said more seriously, "We can't avoid it any longer: One of us has to call him to help."

"I know. Mrs. Reg and Lisa's mother were bugging her, but Lisa really doesn't want to, so I told her I would," Stevie said.

"That's nice of you, especially when Lisa has so much work to do," Carole said.

For some reason the response irked Stevie. "We have a lot of work, too, Carole," she said. "We did those signs all afternoon. Plus I've got a French test in a week, you know."

"I know, Stevie," Carole replied. "It's hard for all of us right now. Anyway, I've got to hang up soon."

The girls chatted for a few more minutes, but neither one of them wanted to prolong the conversation. When they hung up, Stevie felt restless. She'd studied her French for more than an hour already. Besides, she was still on vacation. She stared at the phone, trying to think up something fun to do. After a minute she giggled to herself. She opened her desk drawer, rummaged around a bit, and found an old list of Horse Wise phone numbers. *Atherton* was the first name on the list. Hoping the number would be the same, Stevie dialed it.

"Hello?" a deep voice said.

"Is this the Athertons'?" Stevie inquired.

"Yes, it is," said the voice.

"Could I please speak with your son?" Stevie asked.

The voice started to laugh. "Sorry, I don't have a son. And if this is some kind of telemarketing thing, forget it! My parents never buy anything over the phone."

Stevie didn't understand. She had reached the Athertons', and somebody who sounded like Simon's father had answered. "Excuse me, I'm trying to reach Simon Atherton. Maybe you could tell me—"

"Simon? Why didn't you say so? This is he."

"This is who?" Stevie demanded.

"This is he—I mean, it's Simon."

"It's *you*?" Stevie fairly cried.

"Yes, it is I," said the voice.

It took Stevie a minute to gather her thoughts. The Simon Atherton she knew had a whiny, squeaky voice higher than her own. This Simon Atherton had a low voice. He sounded old. But he did have good grammar. Chad, Stevie's brother, would have said, "This is him" and "It is me." Simon had said, "This is he" and "It is I." So "he" had to be—well—him!

"*Simon?* This is Stevie Lake. Stevie from Horse Wise."

"Oh, hello, Stephanie," Simon said.

Stevie relaxed. That sounded like Simon, too: Simon always called her by her full name. "Simon, how are you? You sound so different!"

"That's what everyone says. Puberty, I guess, Stephanie. How are you?" he asked.

Stevie giggled. Only Simon would use a word like *puberty.* "I'm okay, Simon. I'll tell you why I'm calling." Briefly Stevie explained the dire state of Horse Wise, the bake sale, and the recent effort to recruit members.

"I know all about it," Simon said. "Mrs. Reg filled me in today. And I think I saw you and your friend Carole Hanson working on posters for the bake sale, didn't I?"

"You did? You were at the stables today?" Stevie asked. "Why didn't I see you?"

"You looked so busy that I didn't want to intrude. I simply went for a ride and then did a few chores for Mrs. Regnery," Simon explained.

"Oh. I see," said Stevie, although she didn't, really. The Simon she knew would have come right up and started talking her ear off, intrusion or no intrusion.

"Listen, Stephanie, it's great to talk with you. I'd be happy to help out with the bake sale. Perhaps I could hang up some posters for you. I wish I could talk longer, but I've got a friend coming over to study with me, so I really ought to go. Do you want to meet me sometime to give me the posters?"

Half dazed, Stevie managed to say, "Sure. How about next week?"

"Fine. I'll talk to you then. Good night."

"Night," Stevie said. After putting the receiver down, Stevie found herself staring at it again. One thing was clear: Simon Atherton had changed in Texas. He still used formal, proper English when he spoke, but he sounded older somehow, more confident. Was it just puberty, as he had said? You couldn't judge a person over the phone, Stevie reminded herself. That would be like judging a book by its cover—wouldn't it?

CAROLE FELT STRANGE walking into the Willow Creek Mall by herself. She hated shopping, so she usually avoided the place entirely. When she did go, it was usually because Lisa and Stevie dragged her. But today she had three reasons for being there, and one reason for being there alone. The main reason she had come was to hang up posters for the bake sale. It was hard to believe, but the sale was only two days away. Today was Thursday, tomorrow was Friday— the day she and her father had set aside for the after-school bake-a-thon—and Saturday was the sale. Carole's father had dropped her off at the mall on his way to the grocery store. He was making a special trip to pick up all the stuff they would need to make the cookies.

It was also hard for Carole to believe that her New Year's resolution was now more than a week and a half old. And that was the other reason—the other two reasons—she'd come to the mall: to get away from all the junk food at home, and to pick up some alternative snacks at the new health food store. She hadn't wanted to come with Lisa and Stevie because then she would have had to mention their resolutions, too. Lately there seemed to be an understanding among the three of them that the subject was taboo. It made conversation hard. Carole had to be careful not to mention Veronica or embroidery, and she'd noticed that Stevie and Lisa never discussed food in her presence. But bringing up the subject would start an argument as to whose resolution was hardest.

All in all, Carole felt pretty good about hers. In her head she'd changed it from "I will not eat junk food" to "I will try to eat less junk food and more healthy food." Since the change, she'd hardly cheated at all. Okay, maybe a few handfuls of popcorn. And an old bag of sour cream potato chips she'd found in her desk at school. And there was also the doughnut for breakfast two days ago. But basically, Carole thought with pride, she'd kept her resolution. And that was what counted.

Armed with masking tape and a pile of posters, Carole walked the length of the mall, hanging up signs:

INDULGE YOUR SWEET TOOTH AND SUPPORT YOUR LOCAL PONY CLUB. COME TO THE HORSE WISE PONY CLUB BAKE SALE. THIS SATURDAY, 11:00 A.M. TO 5:00 P.M., AT THE WILLOW CREEK SHOPPING CENTER.

According to Lisa, who'd heard from her mother, there was going to be plenty of baked goods. They'd also managed to find volunteers for Saturday. All of the parents of The Saddle Club were coming, except Lisa's father, who was going to be away on business until Saturday night. Mrs. Reg was also planning to help. Carole's only fear was that even with the sale money, they wouldn't be able to convince Max to keep the club alive. Despite calling everyone they could think of, The Saddle Club hadn't had much luck recruiting new members or convincing old members to rejoin. So far, Simon Atherton was one of the few takers. But what was truly bothering Carole was a nagging feeling she'd had all week. She felt like a hypocrite. How could she convince people to join the Horse Wise Pony Club when The Saddle Club was falling apart at the seams?

After both levels of the mall were plastered with bake-sale signs, Carole checked the mall layout plan to find The Health Nut. Walking there, she passed a cute little coffee shop that had also recently opened. A few people were sitting at the tables reading or talking. Carole hardly ever drank coffee, but suddenly she thought a café au lait or a cappuccino might taste good. Now that she was abstaining from junk food, she found she was more willing to try new things. She studied the complex menu and decided to try a café mocha. Waiting for her drink, Carole looked around the café, checking it out as a possible backup hangout for The Saddle Club. It wasn't likely, but maybe they would get sick of TD's one of these days. This place looked kind of fun. But then Carole saw something that changed her mind. Or, rather, she saw some*one*. Seated at a table for two was Veronica diAngelo. If *she* hung out at the café, then there was no way The Saddle Club would. Hoping to avoid Veronica, Carole quickly paid for her drink. It was too late. As she turned to go, Veronica turned in her seat and saw her. Carole forced herself to stroll over.

"Hi, Veronica. What are you doing here?" Carole asked, trying to be pleasant.

"I came to spend my Christmas gift certificates," Veronica said. Carole looked down and noticed a pile of shopping bags at her feet. "But I'm meeting someone in ten minutes, so I really don't have time to talk, Carole."

"Me either," Carole said loudly. "I have to go finish postering for the Horse Wise bake sale." It wasn't really the truth, since she was basically finished, but she wanted to get a dig in at Veronica for not helping more.

Veronica gave Carole a condescending look. "We all do what we can, don't we? Isn't that nice that you're spending an afternoon hanging up your little signs? Of course, my father is donating a helicopter ride to be raffled off on Saturday. I'm sure it will bring in more money than all of your home-baked chocolate chip cookies combined."

Carole felt her face getting hot. "Are you going to be there Saturday?" she asked testily.

112

"I'm sure we'll show up at some point," Veronica said airily.

"We? You mean your parents are coming?" Carole asked incredulously. She simply couldn't picture the snobby, ultrarich diAngelos standing behind a table selling baked goods.

Veronica seemed to falter. "I—no. No, my parents aren't coming. They have better things to do."

"Oh, well, then I guess I'll see you Saturday," Carole said, seizing a chance to hurry out of the café.

As she headed toward the health food store, Carole had a sudden flash of sympathy for Stevie. Her resolution was tough, there was no doubt about it. It seemed as if every encounter with Veronica turned into a contest.

Inside The Health Nut, Carole was distracted by the wide array of food. There were fat-free chips, PowerBars, energy bars, protein powder, and soy products, not to mention the largest assortment of vitamins Carole had ever seen. "Nutrient-rich ground meal made from Dead Sea algae," Carole read off the back of one of the packages. "Do you eat this or wear it?"

"I think you shampoo with it, actually," said a voice.

Carole looked up, giggling. A tall, blond boy about her age was standing there. "Are you serious?" she asked.

"Unfortunately, yes. My mom buys the stuff in bulk," he said.

"Boy, my dad wouldn't touch any of this stuff with a ten-foot pole," Carole said. She liked the looks of the boy and felt like continuing the conversation. He had deep blue eyes and a friendly smile.

"You don't say? My mother is just the opposite: She prefers health food, health hair care—health, health, health!" he said.

"Gosh, maybe you could help me, then. I came to buy a few snacks that aren't junk food, but I don't know where to begin," Carole confessed.

"It would be my pleasure to assist you," said the boy.

"Great, I—" Carole stopped suddenly. She looked sharply at the boy. There was something about the way he spoke that had given her the oddest sense of déjà vu.

"Is something the matter?" the boy asked.

Embarrassed for staring, Carole apologized. "I'm sorry—I should introduce myself. I'm Carole Hanson."

"But, Carole, don't be silly. I already know you,"

the boy said with a laugh. "Don't you remember me? I'm Simon Atherton."

"You're *who*?" Carole cried.

IF THERE WAS one thing Stevie detested, it was having to spend an afternoon with her brothers. She usually avoided them by going to Pine Hollow, but today her father had put his foot down. She was to come home and study directly after putting up posters for the bake sale. Now that Stevie had passed her French retake, Mr. Lake didn't want her getting behind again. Even the fact that Stevie had beaten Veronica by two points hadn't carried any weight. "But she had a private tutor!" Stevie had protested.

"And what do you call Lisa Atwood?" Mr. Lake had countered.

So, after going to the library, the town hall, and the two banks, Stevie had had no choice but to proceed to enemy territory. Enemy territory was how she thought of her house when Chad, Alex, and Michael were all at home.

Of course, Fenton Hall and Pine Hollow were also enemy territory now, too, on account of Veronica. All week Stevie had tried to avoid Veronica, and all week she had run into her everywhere she went. Luckily, Veronica had seemed distracted each time they met. She would show off whatever new Christmas outfit she happened to be wearing and then disappear. So Stevie had kept her resolution perfectly—or almost perfectly. Okay, she had snapped at Veronica a few times. And she had started a couple of harmless rumors at school about Veronica's hair being dyed. And maybe she had tried to get her in trouble with Miss Fenton for her overdue library books. But all in all, she'd been extremely nice to her.

Stevie hadn't even confronted her with the tack room incident. She couldn't figure out a way to do it without kicking, screaming, and attempting murder. "But just wait till this month of resolutions is up, Miss diAngelo," Stevie muttered ominously to her French book. "Then you'll find out what happens to those who cross Stephanie Lake."

According to Lisa, Mrs. Reg understood perfectly what had happened, but if she did, then why didn't she say something?

"Oh, Stevie, lovely sister dear?" Alex whined outside her bedroom door.

"Go away!" Stevie yelled. For good measure she added, *"Tu es stupide!"*

"You think I'm stupid?" Alex said. "Be careful, or I'll tell on you to Phil!"

"Tell on me for what?" Stevie demanded, putting her French book down on her desk.

"For dating other guys," Alex said.

"You really are stupid," Stevie yelled, annoyed by Alex's dumb comment. "Or crazy. Probably both."

"I am? Then who's your date I see walking up the driveway?"

"Date?" Stevie murmured. "Who could possibly—?" All at once, Stevie remembered. She flung open the door and ran past the astonished Alex. With all of her own postering to do, she'd completely forgotten that Simon Atherton had volunteered to come to her house to pick up his posters.

"Stevie has a new boyfriend! Stevie has a new boyfriend!" Alex followed her down the stairs, taunting her.

"Whoa, Stevie," said Chad, coming out from the kitchen, his mouth full of grilled cheese sandwich.

"Chad, that's disgusting, and I don't have a new boyfriend! Please! Would you give me a little credit? Do you think I'd date a guy like Simon Atherton?" Stevie hissed.

The doorbell rang. Stevie's youngest brother, Michael, appeared out of nowhere to answer it.

"He doesn't look that bad," Chad said, peering through the window.

"Be quiet!" Stevie whispered. "The poor guy is awkward. Very, very awkward. Don't make it worse for him, okay? Let *me* do the talking! Got it?" Pasting a smile on her face, Stevie flung open the door. Then she stopped. Her jaw dropped. The pile of posters she was carrying fell to her feet. Behind her, Stevie's brothers snickered.

Simon smiled politely. Stevie stared rudely. She couldn't think of a single thing to say. Simon Atherton was utterly gorgeous.

"Ow!" LISA CRIED. It was late in the afternoon, almost dinnertime, and she had just pricked her finger for the third time. "Mrs. Reg!" she called. "Look what I've done!"

Mrs. Reg came hurrying from the kitchen with her apron on. "I pricked my finger and it's bleeding!" said Lisa.

"Let me get a bandage! Does it hurt badly?"

"Hurt? Oh, I don't care about that. But the blood is staining the material!" Lisa wailed. She held up a partially finished napkin for Mrs. Reg to see.

"Where? I can't even see it," Mrs. Reg said.

Lisa pointed to a minuscule orange spot on the white linen.

"Give me that," Mrs. Reg commanded. She took the napkin, dabbed at it with her sponge, and handed it back. "There. Good as new."

Lisa thanked Mrs. Reg, picked up her needle, and started in again. She had come over right after school for a marathon embroidery session. After working hard all week on the sampler, learning stitches and practicing them, Lisa had started the napkin set a couple of days before. She had finished one napkin and was now on her second. Mrs. Reg had helped her with the design. They said U.S.P.C. in gray and green, the Horse Wise colors. The border, in brown, was supposed to look like a bridle rein. It actually looked like nothing more than a long, brown line, but Lisa couldn't go back and fix it now.

"Mrs. Reg?" Lisa said suddenly, looking up from the pattern. Mrs. Reg had remained in the doorway, watching Lisa with an anxious look on her face.

"Yes, dear?"

"I'm not going to finish the tablecloth, am I?"

"No, Lisa."

"I'm not even going to start it, am I?"

Mrs. Reg shook her head.

Lisa sniffed. She had worked so hard and now she

was going to fail. She felt tears well up in her eyes. "In fact, I'll be lucky if I get through this napkin by Saturday. Why don't I learn? I always try to do more than I have time for! Now I'll let Horse Wise down!"

Mrs. Reg put an arm around Lisa's shoulders. "Now, now, Lisa. That's not true. You'll have the napkins for Horse Wise. They're beautiful."

"But if I had learned faster . . . ," Lisa sobbed.

"You learned embroidery faster than anyone I know," Mrs. Reg said sternly.

"But what will we do for a tablecloth Saturday?"

"We'll buy paper tablecloths for heaven's sakes. Nobody cares one bit! People come to buy the goodies—they don't even notice what's covering the table." Mrs. Reg patted Lisa's hair comfortingly, but Lisa could not stop sobbing. She couldn't even tell Mrs. Reg the whole truth about why she was upset—that now she was sure to lose the resolution bet. Carole and Stevie would say she had copped out. Sure, she had learned embroidery, but she hadn't produced the tablecloth.

The doorbell rang and Mrs. Reg stood up to get it. Lisa wiped her eyes on her sleeve and tried to compose herself. She was too distracted to pay much attention to who was at the door. She heard Mrs.

Reg greet someone, talk a couple of minutes, and then head back toward the living room. Knowing she should try to be polite, Lisa put down her napkin and looked up expectantly, ready to greet whoever it was.

"I told Simon you were here and he wanted to come in and say hello, Lisa," Mrs. Reg announced, ushering her guest into the room.

"Hello, Lisa," said a tall boy who looked a little like Simon Atherton but couldn't possibly be.

Lisa grinned idiotically. "You—you turned into a swan!" she exclaimed.

Simon blushed red to the tips of his ears. "I did get contact lenses, and my braces are gone," he mumbled.

And you grew five inches and filled out and got a nice haircut and changed from the nerdiest boy in Willow Creek to one of the cutest, Lisa thought. Remembering her manners, Lisa thanked Simon for all of the help he was contributing to Horse Wise. "Stevie told me you were going to poster and to bake something for Saturday. Are you coming, too?"

"I wouldn't miss it for the world," Simon said.

"All right, Simon, we'd better let Lisa get back to her embroidery. She's got a deadline to meet," said Mrs. Reg.

"Yes, I should finish this napkin I'm working on," Lisa agreed. "Or else—" All of a sudden Lisa's heart started beating very fast. Her mouth grew dry. "Or else, nothing!" she cried. "Mrs. Reg, I don't know if I will finish this napkin. Heck, I've already broken my resolution by not finishing the tablecloth. Boy, did I break that resolution. You saw me, Mrs. Reg. I wanted to finish it, but I couldn't, could I? But who cares? Stevie and Carole and I had a little bet over who would break her New Year's resolution first, and I sure lost. Yes sirree, I'm the big loser. Oh, well— you win some, you lose some, right? And now I'll just have to take what's coming to me. Okay, Mrs. Reg, I guess I'll call my mother to come pick me up now. No sense embroidering all night, is there?"

Mrs. Reg and Simon stared at Lisa as she gathered up her things with lightning speed. Simon was the first to find his voice. "Lisa, if it's a ride home you desire, my mother is waiting in the car outside and we could drop you off."

Lisa beamed. That was just the invitation she'd been hoping for. "Wonderful, Simon. I'd love to get a ride with you—if it's not too much trouble."

Mrs. Reg watched Simon walk Lisa out to the waiting car. "Funny how certain breeds mature slower than others . . . ," she murmured to herself.

123

* * *

WHEN LISA GOT HOME she ran to the phone. She picked up the receiver and was about to punch in a number when her mother appeared.

"Lisa, I need to talk to you about a few last-minute details for Saturday."

"Mom, can it wait?" Lisa asked, her hand hovering over the push buttons. "I have to call Stevie and Carole right away."

"Oh, that reminds me. They both called you," Mrs. Atwood said.

Lisa put the phone down. "They did? Did they leave a message?"

"Yes, they left two messages, actually. And the messages were rather strange." Mrs. Atwood pulled a piece of paper out of her pants pocket. "Let's see . . . here we go: Stevie called to tell you she just couldn't hold out any longer. She was very, very mean to Veronica in school today. She wanted me to emphasize the *very*. And Carole said that she hated to have to tell you, but she ate ten bags of potato chips and cheese popcorn this afternoon. Funny messages to leave, wouldn't you say?"

"Mom, you didn't tell them where I was, did you?" Lisa asked breathlessly.

"Yes, I did, dear." Lisa's mother leaned over and

124

gave her a hug and kiss. "I told them that you were at Mrs. Reg's working on your embroidery, that you'd been there all day, and that I was thrilled that my daughter would learn a craft just to please me."

"Mom!" Lisa wailed, her plans ruined. "How could you?"

THE DAY OF the bake sale was bright and seasonably cold. "It's as crisp as my molasses cookies," declared Mrs. Atwood, taking two tins from her bag. "Good weather is always such a promising sign, isn't it?"

Lisa nodded grimly. The sunny day had done nothing to dispel the black mood she was in. She and her mother had arrived early to get ready for the sale. But as she set up card tables and covered them with paper tablecloths, Lisa felt more like she was getting ready for war. The strange thing was, though, this was a war she was determined to lose! She was going to be the one to call Simon Atherton

126

for a date, no matter what Stevie and Carole thought.

The first thing Lisa had to do was finish making a notice about the helicopter ride over Washington, D.C., which the diAngelos had indeed donated. They were going to sell raffle tickets for the ride at a dollar apiece. At five o'clock, when the sale ended, Veronica was going to announce the winner.

By quarter to eleven, a large number of Pony Clubbers and parents had arrived with their baked goods, including Carole and Colonel Hanson and Stevie and her parents. Finishing her sign, Lisa said hello to her friends. The girls hadn't seen each other on Friday, because they'd all been home cooking for the bake sale. But instead of talking a mile a minute, the way they usually did—especially after not seeing each other for a day—the girls kept their greetings short.

"Did you get my message?" Stevie asked coolly.

"Yes," said Lisa, noncommittally, keeping one eye peeled for Simon Atherton.

"Did you get mine?" said Carole, glancing over her shoulder.

"Yes."

"Come on, girls. You can chitchat later. There's work to be done," Mrs. Atwood said. All three of them jumped at the chance to help, glad for the distraction. Mrs. Atwood instructed them to write out price lists, sort change, and tack up directional arrows on telephone poles near the shopping center.

"Let's split up," Lisa said at once.

"That's what I was going to suggest," Stevie said defensively.

"So was I!" Carole attested. "But first," she added, "I want to finish this bag of chocolate-covered potato chips that I've been eating *all week*." With that, Carole reached into the snack bag and crammed a handful into her mouth.

Stevie put her hands on her hips, hazel eyes flashing. She wasn't going to let Carole lose the bet that easily! "Do you have a pen, Carole?" she asked.

Carole shook her head.

"Darn! I wanted to write a hate letter to Veronica first thing this morning," Stevie said loudly. "The way I did *last Saturday*."

"Gosh, you've been busy!" Lisa said, feigning admiration. "I wish I could have gotten that much accomplished. But I haven't done a thing since—since Christmas break ended. So much for embroidering a tablecloth! Ha! Was that ever a joke!"

Overhearing Lisa's last remark as she arrived,

Mrs. Reg came over and joined the girls. "Now, Lisa, I don't want you to be unfair to yourself. You worked very hard. And you know how to embroider now. You can make the tablecloth some other time. For now, the napkins are a marvelous accomplishment."

Stevie giggled as Lisa turned red. "And Stevie," Mrs. Reg continued, "I wanted to thank you for not tattling on Veronica. You've gone out of your way to be nice to her, and don't think it wasn't noticed by both me and Max. Say, those look good," Mrs. Reg said, eyeing Carole's chips. "You're finally dropping the health kick, huh?"

"Aaaargh!" cried The Saddle Club in unison as they split up. Trust Mrs. Reg to expose them all!

DESPITE THEIR FEUDING, the girls had finished the tasks Mrs. Atwood had assigned by eleven sharp. The owner of Sights 'n' Sounds came and unlocked the door of his electronics store in the shopping center. "Save a brownie for me!" the man called.

"Will do," Mrs. Atwood promised. She turned to the Pony Club group. "All right, everyone, this bake sale is now open for business."

It was dead quiet for about five minutes. The riders and parents stood around with nothing to do. And then, all at once, the rush started.

"How much for two of these brownies?"

"Can I get a half dozen muffins?"

"I used to be in Pony Club when I was little. I'll take a piece of chocolate cake."

"Where's the change? I need more quarters!"

"Give me two raffle tickets—no, make it three."

"Are we out of chippers or not?"

"Excuse me, but didn't your daughter once ride in Horse Wise? Do you think—"

"Mrs. Atwood, help! I added this wrong!"

The minutes, then the hours, ticked by. Supplies dwindled. First they ran out of cookies. Then brownies. But the crowd in front of the table got bigger and bigger. People came to shop, stayed to buy a treat or a raffle ticket, and ended up adding their children's names to a Horse Wise mailing list. Nobody seemed to mind the cold weather. With the sun out, it was almost pleasant. Many of the parents had brought hot chocolate or coffee in thermoses, which they shared with everyone. At one table Carole led a discussion about the benefits of learning to ride in Pony Club. At another Mrs. Atwood stuffed envelopes full of cash. The biggest surprise was that

Max, knowing nothing about the bake sale, came to the shopping center and found his Pony Club fundraising and recruiting at full tilt. "Keep up the great work!" he urged Mrs. Atwood and the volunteers, clearly delighted.

Looking at her mother during a rare free minute, Lisa felt a pang of guilt. She had worked so hard to get everything and everyone organized. True, she had loved the sampler that Lisa had given her. But Lisa wished that she, Carole, and Stevie could bury the hatchet in honor of the sale. Out of the corner of her eye, she saw the enthusiastic expressions on their faces as they chatted with customers. For too long, things hadn't been right between them. And Lisa knew why. All at once, she made up her mind. She was going to go over to them and say, "Let's forget we ever made resolutions in the first place, okay?" She turned and crashed right into Simon Atherton.

"Sorry I'm late, Lisa. I was waiting for—"

Like hawks over prey, Stevie and Carole were on them in a second. "Simon, how are you?" Carole asked, bursting in.

"Excuse me," Stevie interrupted, "but I saved a place for Simon at my table."

"Did you, Stevie? Because my mother is running this bake sale, and she told me that Simon is supposed to work with me!" Lisa snapped.

"I'll bet," Stevie said sarcastically. "I'll just bet she did!"

"Do you guys want to have your fight somewhere else?" Carole demanded. "Because Simon and I are here to help Horse Wise Pony Club!"

"So, now *you're* claiming him, too!" Lisa spat. "Even though he liked me first!"

None of the girls noticed Simon turn red and slip quietly away, for in a matter of minutes, the sparring turned into full-out war. The girls stood there, a few feet from the table, and screamed at one another.

"It's all your fault, Lisa!" Stevie yelled. "You started the whole thing!"

"Me?" Lisa cried.

"Yes, you!"

"Stevie's right! You thought up the resolutions!" Carole said accusingly.

"You thought up mine!" Lisa shot back. "And you didn't have to agree to do them in the first place!"

"You pressured us into it!" Carole cried.

"Lisa wasn't the only one! Both of you ganged up on me!" Stevie shrieked.

"No, both of *you* ganged up on me!" Lisa wailed. "I was just trying to help you improve yourselves!"

"Maybe we don't feel like we needed improving!" Stevie barked. "You're the overachiever, not us!"

"Speak for yourself, Stevie! I liked my resolution!" Carole yelled.

"Probably because you cheated on it a million times!"

"That's not fair! You cheated on yours, too!"

The three of them paused to breathe. And in the second they stopped yelling at one another, something became painfully clear. The entire bake sale—the Pony Clubbers, the mothers, the fathers, the residents on their way to or from the stores, Mrs. Reg, Max, Veronica, and Simon Atherton—were all staring at The Saddle Club in horror, fascination, and disbelief.

More embarrassed than they had ever been in their lives, Stevie, Lisa, and Carole froze in their places. They didn't dare move. An excruciating minute elapsed. Then Simon Atherton rose to the occasion. "As we always say," he told the crowd, "Pony Club forms great friendships."

When the laughter died down, Simon waved his hands for silence. "Speaking of friendships, I'd like to introduce you to a very special friend of mine.

Veronica, will you come up and announce the raffle winner?"

"I'd love to, Si," cooed Veronica. She sashayed over to the table and squeezed Simon's hand. The Saddle Club stared at them and then at one another in shock.

"Let's see . . . it's number two-twenty. Number two-twenty? Oh, wait a minute. How silly of me," Veronica giggled. She reached into her pocketbook and took out an entire book of raffle stubs. "That's one of the tickets I bought! I won my very own raffle!"

As the crowd began to clap uncertainly, Simon leaned over and gave Veronica a kiss on the cheek. "Did you hear that ladies and gentlemen? My girl-friend won the raffle!"

At five of nine the next morning, Lisa, Carole, and Stevie arrived at Pine Hollow with their parents. Mr. and Mrs. Atwood, Colonel Hanson, and Mr. and Mrs. Lake began chatting happily right away. The three girls hung back and kept their eyes to the ground. None of them dared look at the others as they walked behind their parents to the tack room.

Posted on the door of the room was a note that said,

HORSE WISE MEETING MOVED TO THE INDOOR RING.

"That's good news!" Mrs. Atwood exclaimed. Still silent, the girls followed their parents to the indoor ring, where they joined the large group of families assembled for the meeting. Mr. Lake grabbed folding chairs from against the wall and handed them to the others. Carole began to set her chair up next to her father, but Colonel Hanson said loudly, "I know you kids want to sit together, so you go on with Stevie and Lisa."

Stevie's and Lisa's parents jostled them and edged them out of the parental row, so the girls had no choice but to set their chairs up next to one another. Once seated, Lisa began to examine her nails intently. Stevie stared at the cobwebs in the rafters. Carole waved hello to the other Pony Clubbers. They were all grateful when Max called the meeting to order at nine on the dot.

"Welcome to this special Sunday meeting of Horse Wise," Max began. "Now I understand why so many Horse Wise members were eager to get out of yesterday's meeting early! The bake sale, as you all know by now, was a huge success. To every parent and child who fit time into their busy days to bake or sell, thank you!" He paused, a twinkle in his eye. "I haven't eaten this many sweets since I raided my mother's cookie jar! And three hundred dollars—" Max waited as the crowd whooped and cheered before continuing. "Three hundred dollars is a great beginning for our spring season. A fantastic beginning. We—or I should say, you—also raised two hundred dollars raffling off the helicopter ride. I'd especially like to thank the diAngelos for that generous donation."

"Yeah, my mother told me that Veronica bought a hundred tickets herself!" Lisa muttered.

"Doesn't surprise me," Stevie said automatically.

"Me either," whispered Carole. "She had to make sure she could win and take Simon."

"Hey," Stevie ventured nervously, "does this mean we're talking to one another again?"

"Shhh!" said a parent in front of them.

For once Lisa was glad for the reprimand. It saved her from having to respond to Stevie. She didn't know what to say. She couldn't stay *not* talking to her best friends, but part of her was still upset about the fight. Why couldn't Stevie and Carole have realized that she was only trying to help them? She focused her eyes back to the front of the ring. Max, she noticed, looked as awkward as she felt. She waited as he cleared his throat several times. Finally

Max said quickly, "I guess it's nice that Veronica diAngelo was, ah, also the lucky winner of the raffle."

"Nice," Lisa murmured, suddenly understanding Max's embarrassment, "and shocking to everyone else! And yes," she added hesitantly, eyeing Stevie warily, "I guess we are talking."

"So, do you see what I see?" Stevie whispered, pointing. Lisa and Carole looked. Ten feet in front of them, Veronica and Simon were sitting on folding chairs, holding hands!

As Max continued praising the Pony Club's recent efforts, The Saddle Club relaxed the tiniest bit. It was clear from what he said that, despite their ugly fight, the bake sale had been more than enough to convince him to keep Horse Wise going. The members and parents had not only raised money, they had also generated a lot of interest in Horse Wise. Max's phone had been ringing off the hook with parents wanting to make sure their children could join in time for the spring season.

"So let's have a round of applause for Mrs. Atwood!" Max concluded. The crowd clapped loudly. "Mrs. Atwood, I was completely in the dark until I happened to show up yesterday, but a little bird told me that you're the one who thought of the bake sale and got everyone interested and ran the thing, too. Great job!" Lisa stole a glance at her mother. Mrs. Atwood looked pleased and was busy brushing off the praise and trying to quiet the applause.

When Max finished, a few of the parents stood up and expressed their new commitment to supporting the club. They had enjoyed getting to know one another during the past two weeks and were eager to stay involved. Almost everyone who spoke mentioned Mrs. Atwood's name to praise her organizing skills.

"This is off the subject," said Mrs. McLean, after a few minutes, "but I was wondering: Colonel Hanson, could I get your recipe for double-chocolate chippers?"

"Me too!" Mrs. Reg called.

"I want to know what you add to your oatmeal cookies, Mrs. Reg!" Stevie's mother spoke up.

As the meeting degenerated into a recipe-swapping session, Stevie, Lisa, and Carole drifted out of the ring. None of them wanted to talk to anyone at the meeting, they were so ashamed of their fight the day before. They didn't want to meet the curious stares of the other Pony Clubbers. They didn't want Mrs. Reg to tell them a story, even if it did have a point. They didn't want Max to make a blunt remark about behaving themselves in public. They didn't want their parents to watch them to see if they were getting along again. And, more than anything, they didn't want to see Veronica and Simon holding hands!

Outside, though, the silence was deafening. Stevie picked up some snow and let it fall from her hands. Lisa folded her arms across her chest. Carole wished the TD's waitress would appear out of nowhere and say, "Wha's a matter? Cat got your tongues?" Even that would be better than not talking. Thinking of the waitress and their last visit to TD's made Carole clench her hands into fists. If only she had said something then, they never would have kept the resolutions, they never would have had the fight, and everything would be normal. Hardly thinking, she packed some snow into her hands, just to have something to do with them. The snow was cold and soothing. Suddenly Carole straightened up. She eyed Lisa. "Say, Lisa?"

"Yes?" Lisa turned.

"New Year's resolutions were the worst idea you've ever had!" Carole yelled, shattering the silence. Without stopping to think, she formed the snow into a snowball and hurled it at Lisa.

As the snow broke on her jacket, Lisa's face froze in shock.

"Lisa, I didn't mean—"

"It's too late for that, Carole!" Lisa shouted. As quick as could be, she made two snowballs and threw them at Carole. Carole missed one by ducking, but the other got her on the back of the neck and the snow slid down inside her jacket.

"Aaahhh!" Carole yelped.

Stevie stood with her hands on her hips, watching Carole prepare to retaliate. "Excuse me? Aren't you two forgetting something? You made me have a resolution!" she cried. "So don't you dare leave me out of this!" Stevie knelt down and began packing snowballs one after another.

Before she could launch one, Lisa gathered a load of snow in her arms and dropped it on top of her. "You didn't have to have a resolution if you didn't want to!" Lisa yelled.

"Well, I felt like I did!" Stevie cried. She was up like a flash, pelting Lisa with her premade ammunition.

"Stop! Stop!" Lisa yelled, her mouth full of snow.

Stevie paused, snowball in hand. "Yes?"

Lisa giggled. "Thanks!" she said, slinging a now perfectly aimed, perfectly formed snowball at

Stevie's upper body. Carole followed suit. In a matter of seconds, the girls were having an all-out snowball fight. They ran and threw and slid and finally shoved one another into the banks of snow left by the plow.

"Why didn't we do this before?" Lisa asked, panting, when Carole and Stevie had wrestled her to the ground.

"I don't know, but I think it would have solved a few problems," Carole said quietly.

"It was like we all wanted to call it quits, but none of us knew how," Lisa said.

"Even you did, Lis'?" Carole asked. She'd assumed that it was easier for Lisa somehow since she had such strong self-discipline.

Lisa nodded. "Especially at the beginning, before Mrs. Reg started helping me. And then when I saw how cute Simon Atherton is now," she kidded, "I *really* wanted to quit!"

Stevie shook her snow-covered head. "I should have known who Veronica's private French tutor was! And who her 'friend' for New Year's Eve was!"

"I should have known who she was waiting for at the mall," Carole said.

"I should have known that 'some breeds mature

more slowly than others'!" Lisa joked. "Mrs. Reg kept trying to tell us."

Carole grinned. "Do you mean to say that if Simon were a horse, he'd be a German warmblood?"

The girls giggled, partly at Carole's joke, but mainly because it was such a relief to be talking and laughing again—to be The Saddle Club again. Lisa was sorry she'd pressured Carole and Stevie into making their resolutions. Stevie was sorry she'd been so competitive that all she'd thought about was winning. Carole was sorry she'd been too nervous—around her own best friends—to say what she really felt. Sometimes after a fight, it wasn't possible to make everything one-hundred-percent perfect, but a simple "sorry" could help clear the air. The three girls took deep breaths. "I'm sorry," they all said in unison.

"No, I'm sorry," Stevie joked.

"No, *I'm* sorry," Carole insisted.

"Well, then—apology accepted," Lisa declared. They all laughed.

Stevie stared up at the winter sky. "It's so great out here. What do you think our parents would say if we went for a quick ride?"

Carole glanced in the direction of the ring. "Do you think they'd even notice?"

Lisa smiled. "We could always make something up about having neglected our horses for the past—oh—ten days or so."

"We have been neglecting them," Stevie said promptly. "All *year*."

"And that goes against everything Pony Club stands for," Carole reminded them.

"That's right," Lisa said, as they retraced their steps and headed toward the tack room. "And why have a Pony Club if you're not going to try to live up to its standards?"

"Why, indeed?" Stevie asked. "That would almost be like—like breaking a resolution."

13

BELLE, STARLIGHT, AND PRANCER were full of energy. Out on the trail, the girls trotted through the brisk air, happier than they had been in days. Eventually they came to a stretch of ground covered with fallen branches. They slowed to a walk.

"I hate to ask this," Carole began, turning in her saddle, "but am I right in thinking that we're hereby forgetting about our res—"

"Don't! Don't even say the word!" Lisa broke in. "I may never embroider another day in my life."

"What are you going to do with the napkins?" Stevie inquired.

"Didn't I tell you?" Lisa asked. "I'm going to give them to Mrs. Reg and Max as a peace offering from The Saddle Club. As soon as I finish the second one, that is."

"So then you are going to embroider at least one more time," Stevie teased her.

Lisa smiled. "Actually, I have to admit I kind of like embroidering. In spite of everything, I'm glad I learned how."

"You know," Carole said thoughtfully, "I think your resolution was the best, Lisa. Whoops! I said the *r* word!"

"That's okay," Lisa responded, "because I think you're right, Carole. I think if I've learned one thing about resolutions, it's that they should be positive and specific. Vague ones don't work because you never know if you're 'cheating' or not. And to be honest, I now think it's harder to stop doing something—like to stop eating junk food—than to *start* doing something."

Carole explained how she had recast her own resolution. "It was easier to try to eat good food than to quit eating bad food. Once I thought about it like that, I actually learned something from my resolution. I convinced my dad to make salads, and I started eating fruit for snacks sometimes instead of chocolate bars. But quitting something just makes you want to do it more."

"You can say that again. I've never wanted to kill Veronica more than I have these past two weeks," Stevie said.

"And I wanted to kill her for you!" Lisa chimed in.

"In the end, Veronica won the day, though, didn't she?" Carole asked reflectively. For once, Veronica had come out smelling like a rose.

"Yes, and I know why," Lisa said. She swallowed hard and then went on, feeling slightly silly but knowing she had to say it. "When the three of us put our heads together, we can always beat Veronica. But we were so busy fighting—the whole time she was sinking her claws into Simon—that we were helpless to stop her. We were so worried about checking up on one another that we forgot to check up on her."

"Don't forget that Simon had something to do with it," Carole said wryly.

"You're right, Carole. Simon must actually like Veronica, too," Stevie remarked.

The girls were silent a moment, trying to comprehend that utterly mystifying fact. None of them could.

"There's no way—"

"It's just too strange—"

"Do you think he lost his brains when he got better looking?" Lisa asked.

"Must be," Stevie said seriously.

"That would explain a lot," Carole agreed.

The girls relaxed in their saddles and loosened the reins a bit so the horses could stretch their necks. "Do you think we'll get in trouble with Max and Mrs. Reg?" Lisa asked, idly stroking Prancer's neck. She hardly cared if they did, now that she and Stevie and Carole were back to normal.

"I doubt it," Stevie said. "But I think we're getting our comeuppance anyway. Mrs. Reg knows how much we detest Veronica. I'll bet she lets Veronica get away with her lie about the tack room."

"Serves us right, I guess," Carole said. "But I feel bad for you, Stevie, since you were the one who cleaned it up."

"Don't," Stevie said. "Sometimes it's good to have an enemy."

"When is that?" Carole asked.

"When it brings friends together," Stevie answered.

None of the girls said anything for several minutes. Each of them was lost in her thoughts, although the thoughts were similar: Strangely enough, they were all silently thanking Veronica for being so awful!

Soon they came to a bend in the trail. There was an opening in the trees. The girls stopped to look out. They could see the roofs of Pine Hollow in the near distance.

"I think we should all make resolutions," Lisa announced.

"*What?*" Stevie and Carole cried.

"I'm serious," Lisa said. "Listen, this is what I mean: I, Lisa Atwood, resolve that when I make resolutions in the future, I'll make them for myself only and not for other people, and I won't bite off more than I can chew."

"Okay, I get it," Carole said readily. She thought for a minute. "I, Carole Hanson, resolve to start eating junk food again, but in moderation when possible. And on movie nights with my dad, I'll ask him to leave off the extra butter."

Stevie looked at her two friends. Lisa's cheeks were flushed pink with the cold air. Carole's eyes were bright. It seemed impossible that less than twenty-four hours ago, she had been so angry at them that she'd been shouting at the top of her lungs. Having fought with them made her realize how lucky she was to have them. The Saddle Club were such good friends, they could weather storms— even storms that started from within.

"I, Stevie Lake," she began, and paused. "I, Stevie Lake, resolve never to make another resolution again, as long as I live."

Carole and Lisa took their hands off their reins for a moment and applauded into the still, winter air. Stevie's resolution was definitely the best.

ABOUT THE AUTHOR

BONNIE BRYANT is the author of many books for young readers, including novelizations of movie hits such as *Teenage Mutant Ninja Turtles* and *Honey, I Blew Up the Kid*, written under her married name, B. B. Hiller.

Ms. Bryant began writing The Saddle Club in 1986. Although she had done some riding before that, she intensified her studies then and found herself learning right along with her characters Stevie, Carole, and Lisa. She claims that they are all much better riders than she is.

Ms. Bryant was born and raised in New York City. She still lives there, in Greenwich Village, with her two sons.

Don't miss Bonnie Bryant's next exciting
Saddle Club adventure . . .

STABLE HEARTS
The Saddle Club #63

The Saddle Club girls are having a blast planning
the Valentine's Day barn dance at Pine Hollow Stables. Then Stevie learns that the dance at her boyfriend's school is on the same night. Now Stevie has
to persuade Phil to ditch his dance and come to hers!

Stevie, Lisa, and Carole also have to keep a new
rider at Pine Hollow out of Mrs. Reg's hair. The last
thing she needs is pesky old Mr. Stowe hanging
around, asking dumb questions. Mrs. Reg has got a
stable to help run and problems to figure out—like
why one of the usually chipper stable ponies seems so
depressed. Can a pony have a broken heart?

It's going to be a whirlwind Valentine's Day for
everyone at Pine Hollow!